certifiable

Also by the author

Hamburger Valley, California
Imagining Baseball: America's Pastime and Popular Culture
Dogboy
Lardcake

certifiable

(fictions)

David McGimpsey

implosion
imprint

INSOMNIAC PRESS

Edited by Stephen Cain

Library and Archives Canada Cataloguing in Publication

McGimpsey, David, 1962-
    Certifiable / David McGimpsey.

ISBN 1-894663-70-5

    I. Title.

PS8575.G48C43 2004   C813'.54   C2004-903969-5

The publisher gratefully acknowledges the support of the Canada Council, the Ontario Arts Council and the Department of Canadian Heritage through the Book Publishing Industry Development Program.

Printed and bound in Canada

Insomniac Press
192 Spadina Avenue, Suite 403
Toronto, Ontario, Canada, M5T 2C2
www.insomniacpress.com

for Kathy

Table of Contents

Foreword

You might be asking, why did I come out of my 18 year retirement to write this book? I'll tell you, it wasn't for the sweet punch my agent serves at his so-called "80s Night" parties. I enjoy the singing along to "Eye of the Tiger" and have been known to pocket a salmon quesadilla or two, but the punch he serves is like 100% gin. How else can I explain going into his dresser and trying on all his socks? No, I wrote this book simply to express life's human despairs and the exhilaration of life's universal joys—like the time my TiVo remembered to tape that rerun of *Felicity* where she finally does it with Ben. That was awesome. I also figured lots of people are still writing books, so why not Davey? Pete Rose wrote a book and maybe I could write one without using the word "baseball" so often—baseball this, baseball that, God, that's really annoying! Of course, lots of things have changed in the world in the last two decades. Personally, I'm surprised woodburning portraits never really came back in style, but who can account for taste? After several tragic misunderstandings of the proper handling of the woodburning "pencil," I confess I became quite prolific in the craft, and though I'm justly proud of my crowning achievement, "Tribute to Posh Spice," I realized it was time to get back to a less fickle, less third-degree burn causing, art. But, my, everything feels different today. Now, apparently, there's more than one kind of aerobics. Step aerobics, power aerobics, couch-bound aerobics, Kenny Loggins lovin' retro aerobics—it is a complicated time. I swear, how people can choose a potato chip, what with the ruffled and non-ruffled brands both being so tasty, I'll never know. But I have decided to meet the hurly-burly of the era with the will of a true believer—for if there is one thing I must do now it is prove all the nay-sayers wrong. Like my old writing teacher who said

Gayly Through the Gloomy Gloaming was "perhaps not the best manuscript title," or my erstwhile co-worker who said I would never be "barista material"—I'll show them, I will show them all. Now I am ready to reap the rewards that invariably await those who write of life, death and a philosophical little gopher named Grady. Make no mistake, I am expecting huge rewards! Like that guy in Oceanside who had his poem "Why Oceanside Rawks" on the bulletin board at the Oceanside *Stop 'N Shop* for nearly a year. Can you imagine? That guy got to go on the *Hello Oceanside* radio show and they gave him, like, a thirty dollar gift certificate at El Pollo Loco. As Grady himself would say, that's living. Maybe, if I'm lucky, I'll be honored with an even more prestigious award from the literary community—like being named the Academy of Country Music's "Entertainer of the Year," an award once shared by Robert Penn Warren and Mel Tillis. You are looking at the next *Oprah* book. My stories of a plucky pioneer who yearns for a lost European lover all the while putting up with the indignities of a small town rhubarb cannery will somehow remind you it's never too late for plastic surgery. After a life of suffering for my art, with the money I make here I might be able to purchase the two things everybody wants in life: Buford Pusser's whoop-ass stick and Buford Pusser's solid gold football. To the future! People are always saying, "Don't tell me, you could write that down—but you should definitely not be telling me." So I have responded to their editorial kindness and I give to you my first effort since ghosting the biography *Rock Me Falco* (Falcobooks, 1986). I hope you enjoy this book, and you too may experience the generous spirit of people who always look me straight in the eye and say, "You're certifiable. Absolutely certifiable."

Rawk!

—DM, Oceanside, CA

B.G.U.

My third unpublished novel, *Big Guy University*, was certainly my worst. Who wants to read a whole book about a guy named Steve? Who wants to read about a guy who finally gets a job as an advice columnist even though he seems ill-equipped to do anything but offer misanthropic commentary like some scraggly Gen X movie hero? And, honestly, who would want to read anything about the girlfriend I had provided for Steve-o; did "Amanda" do anything but make "terrific faji-tas" and insist Steve was really not such a bad guy?

Did I not use words like *jouissance* and *modality*? Did I not pretend, what with Steve's uncanny ability to make people in tollbooths smile, that he was a totally different kind of man than I was?

I was crushed when nobody wanted to read my first novel (*Guy on the Highway*) and pretty much lost my will to live when even my friends wouldn't read through the second (*Ditch-Blessings*), but by the time I started *B.G.U.* I guess I was writing in the same way somebody works on their gardening or on one of those jumbo jigsaw puzzles of Big Ben. It was something to do in the early evenings to help keep an illusion alive.

Unlike the pathetic Steve, I worked in advertising. I was a member of a four person team within a mid-sized east coast company where we were responsible, among other things, for creating a pitch for a new line of thick, deodorant soap called "Engage." A rather unimaginative clichéd product to dedicate my days to, but it was better than checking up on the stock of DVDs at the local Buy Now. Holcomb and Rahlolld was quite successful with local campaigns: a morning radio show famously tagged as "Better than calling in sick!"; a local restaurant chain where it was assured, "The fun is the food at Binty's!"; and a local law firm who told all in the Tri-State area—"Don't pay for *their* mistakes."

My ex-wife wasn't around to see me write *B.G.U.* but she was, she said, "disappointed" I didn't turn out to be a better novelist. She had a tweedy image of me which was flattering but depressingly easy to dismantle. Two years after the divorce, not long after I had made one of the creative teams at H-R she phoned to tell me, with the severity of a judge, how I "lacked character."

I said: "Does this mean I can't expect a drunken call in February wishing me a Happy New Year?"

"You're a fish-faced jerk," she said on more secure, colloquial ground.

Maybe I still cared what she thought, but was happier without her. Aside from the whole getting to watch ESPN in the morning, I made good dough and I had a semi-serious girlfriend who also made good dough as a "fitness consultant." This would make my girlfriend a 24-year-old aerobics instructor named "Terri," which sounds more clichéd than the thick deodorant soap, but there you go. My ex-wife was the kind of person who'd make fun of Terri with an "i" but, let's face it, who wouldn't? It sounded like the kind of girl *B.G.U.*'s Steve would moon over while Amanda perfected her Tex-Mex entrées. But I liked Terri; she didn't take things too seriously and even if she dotted her i's with smiley faces she wasn't an ambitiousless caricature. I don't deny her great cheer—her Courician perkiness—her unfailing willingness to musically assure a group of fatties they should "shake their buns"—but she was possessed of an inner strength that one rarely encounters. Anyway, was I supposed to regret the youthful apple-polish she gave my graying life? Was I supposed to find someone who just liked to sit and talk about shitty movies?

The transition from *aspiring writer* to *full-time hack* is always an uncertain demotion. The pain about artistic failure is nobody comes with a pink slip and says, "I'm sorry, the aspiring writers of America have decided to let you go. We wish you the best of luck with your future endeavors be they involved with hammer, mop, spatula or broom." By the time you realize any of this, the pink slip has already been handed-in and all you have are drawers full of unread manuscripts. Even the dippy Steve of *B.G.U.* knew that. The office of H-R was similarly filled with former *artistes* who now had an intractable cynicism towards all who retained noble aspirations. Rationalizing *everybody is selling something*

was our form of heightened consciousness. Those who thought otherwise were still suckling the very pap we were offering in both original and
lemon-lime formats. And though I fit right into that world, my story
begins before I had finished my contribution to H-R's soap campaign,
because, believe it or not, the story for *B.G.U.* was optioned as a screenplay for an agency and a movie studio which, for legal reasons, I am not
at luxury to name.

How did my stinky manuscript find its way to Hollywood? I wasn't
sure, but I knew it had something to do with my friend John who
worked with an entertainment agency (brazenly called *Star Power*) in
Toronto, Canada. I'd been friends with Toronto John since I met him
at a writer's conference at a southern Vermont university. I'm ashamed
to admit I attended such an obvious cash-bilk and when I talk about
John to my friends I'm careful not to mention we met at the pricey
workshop. These conferences are usually the reserves of talented,
neurasthenic women who are just one bad prescription away from a
stay at another kind of retreat. When I applied to the workshop I had
this delusion I'd meet some literary bow-wow who'd be astonished by
my stuff and would rush me posthaste to meet his or her publisher.
Instead, I became friends with Toronto John who wasn't so ashamed,
but was also coming to terms with his last run at becoming a writer.

Unwilling to put our hearts into the work, we concentrated on
summer-camp fun. That Vermont workshop was a post-adolescent
bonding-fest, replete with put-on questions to famous writers (Toronto
John asked Rick Moody "what are your lucky Powerball numbers?"),
silly-hearted affairs with girls up from the city, drunken threats to piss
on Robert Frost's grave. We laughed at how terrible our pieces were
and mocked the careful critiques these abominations were offered by
the earnest hopefuls. "Can you believe this girl said my story lacked
convincing narration? Christ, it lacked convincing *spelling!*" It was a
defense mechanism: it was also the truth. Perhaps this unflinching part
of Toronto John's nature got him his job at the Star Power agency.

As soon as he answered the phone I asked: "Did you give somebody
my manuscript?"

"Dude!" he laughed; "What one is that?"

"The one about the advice columnist."

"I didn't *read* it, dude, get serious, but, yeah I think I gave it to this guy at *Excellency* in L.A." (Excellency was another idiotically named agency). *"He s*aid he was looking to *develop stuff*. Scripts. Can't remember his name ... something WASPy, but out of the ordinary ... like, *Blueberry*, or *Blankenship*. Remember, pal, don't get feedback, get paid ... Why?"

So, I read him the trouble-starting e-mail I got from Hollywood:

LIKED *BIG-U* V. MUCH—WOULD LIKE TO TALK ABOUT IT—POSSIBLE MOVIE—QUIK $$$

"Wowee," Toronto John said. And then I started blabbing—the real nervous blabbing one would associate with the alternate on a cheerleading squad. I started losing concentration, boring Toronto John with details about the thick deodorant soap campaign, about Terri and, predictably, about the ex-wife. I reflected on how nice it was that we had both gone on in life, with no hard feelings, and how I'd like to think she'd be happy for my recent fortunes and how great it was going to be to rub her sour prune face in it all!

Toronto John listened in on a third line as I talked to the Hollywood guy who sent me the e-mail. He was all-business and straight to it, as if he was handing out money all day: "I liked the manuscript because the guy has quite a few good lines. The story with the wife doesn't interest us too much, but the zingers do. Have you ever thought of writing comedy?"

"You mean like Pauly Shore becomes a rapper?"

"What? What? Please—what about screenplays? Do you have any experience?"

From these few words, these few reasonable suggestions, I managed to convince myself I was finally a writer. Making no distinction between *New Yorker* essayist and someone on call to doctor scripts for *L.A. Law: The Next Generation*, I was on my way. I was sure I was even better than most: *a Hollywood screenwriter* and I was going out there— settling quickly on the $10,000 the agency promised for first-rights, etc.

Terri liked the idea of L.A. so much she wanted to get married. It was a comfort to know we'd be in it together, even if it meant packing boxes and boxes of aerobics gear that might never be opened again—at least not until fashion's next great hot pink explosion. H-R was steamed I wanted to go out west and one of the nits there made some motion they'd sue me for breach of contract. They didn't have much of a case, my lawyer said, but my lawyer would say the people of Valdez, Alaska didn't have much of a case if Exxon was on the line. I left some sketched ideas, some copy and a promise to keep in touch with H-R and to return to the team someday but they all wanted me to just say goodbye. Ray Wedall, the senior member of my team, gave me his best shot: "You know, the moment you step out of here Elinor Chase is taking your desk." Elinor was a legendary advertising sad sack, whose Sherlock Holmes campaign for a lemonade mix ("It's Lemonentary, Dear Watson") was H-R's biggest creative disaster and she was dying to get on a higher profile team. I laughed and told Wedall I didn't care. Like a teenager, I was thinking of escape: of screenplays where the phrase "huge explosion" is repeated and underlined; where cleavage make up was an art on the same scale as the lithograph.

Terri and I moved into a small apartment building in El Segundo. Under the illusion that the film industry was one large branch plant, like the GE Factory in Schenectady, I thought it was too far from "work." I never much noticed the orange trees and rhodedendra which had Terri in rhapsody, but it was all "amazing" for her. It seemed like before she unpacked her little baby blue dumbbells she had a job teaching Pilates at the "Hollymain Dance Studio." She never heard the LAX-bound planes flying overhead and every night, like we were at a summer cottage, she would turn to me and say "can we go get some frozen yogurt?"

The guy on the phone met me for lunch at an Indian restaurant in Century City, had me sign a deal with the agency, gave me a signing check, and left early—perhaps sensing I would need to ask the waiter to pack up all the uneaten food for home. The guy also told me he knew of nobody outside of cartoons with a name like "Blueberry." He said he might have something for me with a script involving Julianna Margulies that was "in big trouble." *I wonder why?* So, like every other boner in Hollywood I waited and waited for my imaginary friend to give me a call about his zinger-less script. I still get jumpy when I hear

Ms. Margulies's name mentioned. Bored, I phoned my ex-wife to let her know where I was and to see if she would, for my amusement, eat her heart out.

"I met Cameron Diaz," I said. "She was all liquored-up."

"Are you getting any writing done?"

"I'm almost there," I said, like a delinquent student. Actually, I had managed to clear space on my desk and figured out how long a *venti latte* lasts when walking the beach.

"What *kind* of writers are out there?" she asked skeptically.

"All the best. John Irving is here working on, uh, *Scooby Doo 3* or something."

"Yeah right," she said.

Irving was her favorite writer. Once, when we seemed in love, she dragged me to see him at some reading venue way downtown. She even brought along several of his books and showed them to me like the bookmobile lady, carefully explaining what each book meant to her. A kind of poetic justice ruled that evening when Irving's handler told the audience that due to the author's preternatural celebrity he would not be signing books. The crowd twittered and exhaled the way golf fans do at that just-missed putt. I wasn't unhappy at all; I could see how she wished I was more like big John and I was glad to have something concrete to slag Garp-boy with.

"I don't want to have this conversation," she said.

"Oh, I gotta go," I said "Terri's taking me running."

"Feel the burn, Chachi," she said.

Chachi?

It wasn't too long before I was on the phone to H-R offering them more "input" vis-à-vis the thick deodorant soap. I wanted a "regular consulting fee" and opened myself up to Ray Wedall's comment "that's great—our regular consulting fee this year happens to be a case of Pepsi." By then, Toronto John had come down to stay with us for a bit while he took care of some L.A.-biz. It was good for Terri because he'd go with her to those stupid dance-clubs up on the Strip that I refused to go to. Meanwhile, I rested at home and started to concoct my fourth unpublished (and still unfinished) novel.

After being relieved of four serviceable jokey scenes, the agency dropped its rights to *B.G.U.* (except those jokey scenes) and, soon after, dropped me.

I did not start the last novel with any sense of its future—that I would learn from the last failures and fix that noise. No, it might as well have been called *B.G.U. Part II: Return of the Bong-Master.*

Every other night, when Terri was teaching or out, I'd walk up to this little Mexican-Chinese restaurant to write things long hand and to eat food that Terri had banished from our lives. The waiter who brought me my plum chicken tacos, Philip Wong, was the only person I have ever talked to about my fourth novel.

"So what's your book about again?" Philip would ask.

"I'm not sure. This guy named Steve and he has this girlfriend . . . Anyways, it's, as they say, a testament to the preference of madness to the durability of perception."

"Who said that, Hamlet?"

"Nah, I think it's something Screech said to Principal Belding."

"And what's next for you?"

"I'll probably go back east sometime and return to the buy-my-pirate-themed-toilet world of advertising. Shiver me timbers, she draws down like a giant squid."

In the novel, "Steve" was in the Valley, always up late at night, full of gin, and it's just him and his late-night TV friends. Soon enough, in a perverse twist on the whole notion of TV and talking horses, Steve starts having conversations about art and aesthetics with Mr. Ed. Anyway, one night, Steve's flipping around and he sees an old episode of *Fame* he hadn't seen before: Bruno's depressed because there's a flashier synth/piano whiz in town and Shorofsky starts beating him with a stick saying "you lost faith in your art!" or at least that's what Steve saw. This plunges him further into aesthetic crisis. Steve flips stations and watches a movie where Michael J. Fox is like a bellhop or something. The Mike Fox character seems to know a Chinese food delivery guy by name.

I never actually read any of this stuff to Philip Wong or anyone. It wasn't about following a dream but betraying it with senseless determination, following the self-pity inherent in being oblivious to failure.

True, if they had Hallmark cards that read "sorry about the desperate inertia," I'd have more mementoes for my office desk now—a way to relate to other people. Like the protagonist in the unfinished *Steve's Pie Shop,* I daydreamed about drizzly fall days back east and about wasting money on magazines. But, by the complex middle part, where it usually falls apart for the amateur writer, I dreaded showing my face back there. Worst thing of all? While Terri-with-an-i aerobicized her way to God knows where, I had gained a lot of weight. It's funny though, the Mexican food out there isn't as good as you might think.

English 318
Walt Whitman and Emily Dickinson   (6 Credits)

This course is a critical introduction to Nineteenth Century Poetry as well as a primer in the terminology concerning "mood-swings," particularly the instructor's. Students will be familiarized with moments where the instructor will be wild-eyed and intent, like a rogue cop who's come face to face with the kind of punk who ruined his faith in America; in fact, the Socratic exchange of the classroom will feel more like clips edited from the final edition of Full Metal Jacket because they "scared the audience too much." The instructor will throw little metal bolts at you, saying "there you go, bacon-hips," and, then, having shared that sense of humor, the instructor will call you friend. The student will have to sit there while the instructor bursts in like an understudy given a big break in Anchor's Away and, after a rousing, dramatic, tap-friendly reading of "To What You Said," will spend class time talking about the wondrous slope of a neighborhood street in October or will ask if anybody's brought a corkscrew. The students will be expected to absorb sarcasm like rain in Las Vegas; when the instructor quotes Whitman's "Brooklyn Ferry" only to brag about lucrative university grants blown by taking weekends in a New York bar called "Old Neck," the students are expected to give this the rapt attention usually reserved for Brian Piccolo's last words.   When the instructor mocks Dickinson's famous "Wild Nights!" by saying "yeah, right, Emily" the students are required to remember the instructor is talking about them.   When the instructor produces the educational puppets, Emmy and Wally, and has them kiss each other, the students are to note this is how it may have been in real life. Like the President, the instructor will use the phrase "make no mistake" quite frequently, as in "make no mistake, there will be more natural disasters in my grade sheet than there are in Bangladesh"; as in, "make no mistake, waiting for me to return corrected papers will make standing in line at the DMV seem like The Minute Waltz." Aside from enriching general knowledge of our two most consistently incomprehensible and iconoclastic writers, the aim of this course is to preserve certain aspects of the class system—at least, the instructor hopes, the aspects which separate professors from the world you feel most comfortable in.

Presley Agonistes

Elvis wants you to be proud of your collection of coffee mugs. Elvis wants you to be okay with the way you talk baby talk with your spouse. You know what I'm talking about. Don't think nobody hears you: *nodgkin, boodgie, moopsy, satnin, sooty-soot.*

A university I once taught at had a reputation for being a little conservative, and its English department for being rigorous in its attention to the teaching of the "landmarks of literature." A bit of this reputation, however, was tested when a colleague of mine was getting some press—not all of it favorable—because he was about to start teaching a course called "Bob Dylan and the Literature of the Sixties." Bob Dylan as literature? "The times they are a-changin' in the ivory towers of learning" led an article in a popular national magazine. I talked to my colleague about this cool Bob Dylan course and I started enthusiastically anticipating a project I hoped to do one day—thinking I'd likely spend my life as a professor. That was, to introduce something about the body of literature about Elvis. Rather than find out we were kindred spirits, the new Professor of Dylanology was taken aback, "Elvis *Presley*?" he said, as if it was somehow possible I was talking about Elvis Grbac or Elvis Costello; "This course will be nothing like *that*!" In other words, Bob Dylan had "made it" into the academy and *deserved* the class. Dylan was over the wall, to the green fields of Flaubert and Walden, while Elvis remained in the trailer park of pop cult crudities along with *The National Enquirer* and *Gomer Pyle, USMC.* Somewhat deflated, I told my colleague how the funniest and most enigmatic thing Elvis Presley ever said in his life was "my mouth's so dry it feels like Bob

Dylan slept in it." Unimpressed by my contribution to his scholarship, my colleague rushed off to a suddenly imminent appointment.

Elvis was really Buddha and he drove in a superpowered aircar so he could go make sandwiches for blind children. "Has anybody been more publicly ridiculed than Elvis Presley?" my lecture notes begin, "Is he not the most dependable synecdoche the intellectual has for his or her superiority to popular culture? Is Elvis not the king of a whole army of things (processed cheese, instant coffee, drinking soda for breakfast, paintings of dogs playing poker, go-karts, Dale Earnhardt cigarette lighters, instant cheesegrits, .45s) the traditional American scholar has posited his whole identity against? Is this why the academy wants to so thoroughly Southernize Elvis—to baptize him in chicken fat, to link him to the hillbillies in *Deliverance* and to newsreels of redneck opponents of Civil Rights? Is this why they're always saying things like "in the South, Elvis is second only to Jesus!"?

Feeling the pinch of students who are no more engaged by Presleyanna than they are by hearing how *Measure for Measure* reads like a tragedy, I move quickly—ahead of the religious parts of my notes. Terrified by the vocal Christian contingent, as well as by the hostile shiftings of students who believe declaring themselves atheist is the most profound thing in the world. Despicable snobbery is, after all, what the school sells, and many of my colleagues, who seemed to me just one conference away from perfecting their phony British accents, wanted to be sure, when they wondered where *it all went wrong,* they'd know to quickly point to the peanut butter-eating fool who tears up when singing "For the Good Times."

A) Elvis's mansion serves as a kind of wailing wall for the banalities of modern life, and is a reasonable measure of working-class remembrance.

B) Whatever tackiness it embodies, regardless of the hundreds of people goofing on Elvis's signature *thank you, thank you very much*, there's a sense of *real feeling* around Graceland and, as one might expect, "a complete absence of pretension." Aesthetically, is authentic hokum preferable to faked earnestness? Given a choice, would you take Elvis's *He's Your Uncle, Not Your Dad* or John Lennon's *Working Class Hero?*

C) G-land. It is a pilgrimage, but a safe one, where the pilgrim is not compelled to have his or her life "changed by the moment."

Until somebody discovers a black velvet painting which turns out to be a self-portrait painted by Elvis Presley, there will never be a "pure product of America." Until then, Elvis wants us all to enjoy the bumper cars, the strawberry milkshakes—and he doesn't care if you die trying.

O the fried banana sandwich! Is there any better sign of Elvis's resting place among us than he got fat eating fried banana sandwiches and taking pills? "You might notice a familiar trope in Elvis lore, like how he took his friends on a private jet to Denver for a peanut butter sandwich, these stories are meant to intimate how Elvis's extravagant opulence arose out of the simplest practicalities."

Q: Why did Elvis wear ridiculously wide belts with lavishly expensive gold buckles?
A: *To keep his pants up!*

At a more undergraduate-orientated football school where I taught a heavy 4-and-4 course load, I led one lecture called *American Novel /American Cinema*, which was a fancy way of saying "you don't have to read the book to pass the course." It wasn't a very glamorous job but, out of necessity, I finally learned how to teach and how to enjoy the company of students. I felt like them: like I was getting away with something, like it it didn't matter if I answered a question with the phrase "uh, I don't know." Anyways, I brought in Elvis's *King Creole* (based on Harold Robbins's *A Stone for Danny Fisher*) and it went over so well I kind of dispensed with the American Novel focus and, by winter, I was bringing in *Paradise Hawaiian Style* and *Kissin' Cousins*. Feeling my own failed ambitions, I talked a lot about how Elvis wanted desperately to be the next James Dean or Marlon Brando and how the traditional reading of the Elvis movie was *pity*—that their "technicolor goofiness was a splashing reminder of the allure of falseness—of latent talent unfulfilled."

The dominant movie image of Elvis, the simp, singing songs like "No Room to Rhumba in a Sportscar," "Smorgasbord" and "The Bullfighter was a Lady"—becomes, for fans, a most pitiful station in the passion of Elvis. Whether or not Elvis would ever have succeeded in terms of "serious" acting is impossible to say. Undoubtedly all soap operas are crowded with actors who believe they'll break out of their current roles as beefy doctors and treacherous ex-wives to become the next Alec Baldwins and Demi Moores. The speculation that Elvis turned down the part Kris Kristofferson played in *A Star is Born* (1976) because "Colonel Parker wanted too much money," is often recalled as the final missed opportunity in Elvis's pathetic screen career. But whether Kristofferson's role would have given him his ultimate "serious" appreciation is doubtful—given the gross-out pretensions of *A Star is Born*, or *Giant* and *East of Eden* for that matter, one might gladly take *Viva Las Vegas*.

In the summer I would smoke pot with some of my A students (even going to one of their parents' swimming pools!). When into the Pabst Blue Ribbon at a student bar called The End Zone Pub, I would admit it had become so difficult, defending American popular culture to my peers since I thought of Elvis's music as an academic *dirty secret* on the same level as a stash of porn or voting Republican. And, in turn, I too grew embarrassed when they thought of me as the "Elvis guy" and not the "Faulkner guy."

The movie which vexed me, practically on a daily basis, was *Viva Las Vegas*—the love story between race car driver Lucky Jackson (Presley) and showgirl Rusty Martin (Ann-Margret).

The plot twists several ways: Lucky wins a big roll at a craps table which is just enough to cover the costs of entering his car in the Las Vegas Grand Prix. On his way to the race, he bumps into sexy Rusty and, heart aflame, he searches all over Vegas for her with another love-struck sap —Lucky's chief rival, the suave Count Elmo Mancini.

When Lucky finally finds Rusty, she pushes him in a swimming pool to cool off his ferocious (but obviously winning) sexual advance. When Lucky falls in the pool, his bankroll falls out of his pocket, which is then picked up by a kid who promptly stuffs the roll into the pool's suction drain.

Day after day I would wonder why Lucky accepted his money was lost so quickly? "It's no use," he says to his best friend Shorty (Nicky Blair); "the money's gone!" Why couldn't Lucky have figured out it was lost in the water and then have management check pipe and drain? Why didn't he ask that kid what it was like to be the stupidest kid in the world? Was it the gambler's need to lose big? Or was it the way it should be? Should I have, similarly, walked away from the academy the first time my thesis advisor told me what makes a really good thesis?

Watching *Viva* on my computer (the digital equivalent of a Yugo), I did not spend all my time suggestively tracing the mouse's pointer over Ann-Margret's most intimate areas! I knew Rusty was trying to make Lucky jealous in consenting to go out with Count Mancini but I wish she didn't and, considering Rusty's refreshingly pro-prostitution showstopper, "Appreciation," in the movie's climactic talent competition, it still bothers me.

Elvis wants you to stop being so cynical about his black belt. For so long his black belt from the Kang Rhee Institute has been questioned in the way a podiatrist's diploma from the University of Aruba might.

"Pantomime karate kicks and chops are the trademark gestures of the late-stage Elvis and a great boon to the legion of his impersonators."

Driving north for an interview ("American Moderns") which I did not tell anybody on my then-current faculty about, I went to Graceland for my very first time. Though I obviously considered myself an Elvis fan, I just couldn't imagine going there, it seemed so carnival-like and so out of the way.

It certainly was not what I expected. By celebrity standards, Graceland is quite *small*. It's a mansion all right, but it's the kind of mansion a successful orthodontist buys for his second wife—certainly not the kind of Malibu palace you'll see in the pages of *In Style* magazine. Renée Zellweger's boathouse is probably as large and luxurious as Graceland. Perhaps the most telling thing about Elvis is he never moved to California.

I found out how tours of Graceland used to be led by these perky Southern hostesses, "the pride of Memphis," who'd patiently inquire of the crowd after every one of their explications, "Now do y'all have any questions about the Jungle Room?"

But now, for reasons which are probably related to cost-cutting and getting people in and out posthaste, they've dispensed with the hostesses and introduced those horrible audio guides. Not only do the audio guides needlessly hurry you, they prevent talking between visitors, and speak to the tourist as if he or she was completely ignorant of the Elvis story. And audio guides do not take questions about the Jungle Room. Perhaps most onerous of all is that the voice on the new audio tour is Priscilla Presley's. Elvis's only wife and current CEO of Elvis Presley Enterprises, Inc. Priscilla's version of life in Graceland moves between the sickeningly sweet and the downright false. I don't think a visit to Elvis's home should be the occasion for the revelation of the most lurid stories in Presleyland, but Priscilla's Disneyfied version of Graceland is so self-aggrandizing you'd never know she and Elvis divorced in 1973. The audio-tour voice certainly does not say "this is the room where I first thought about sleeping with Elvis's karate instructor."

Elvis doesn't want us to be mean to Priscilla, and maybe that's not so hard to do: she has parlayed her Elvis-and-me tale into a billion dollar fortune (even making a TV movie where, to boost ratings, a scene described in her book as *rough sex* is categorically declared *rape*) and has raised Elvis's daughter in such a way she wouldn't be as "spoiled" as she was with her father and the girl could still grow up to be one of Michael Jackson's most impressive wives. And even if Priscilla is giving much of this Elvis-related fortune to the Scientology temple in Los Angeles, at least, unlike Elvis, she's not spending it on Cadillacs that she's handing out like Pez.

He should have lived only so Bruce Springsteen could write songs for him. Wouldn't every Boss song sound better if Elvis did it instead?

Elvis Berry, Elvis Holly, Elvis Spears . . . don't tell me I don't know rock and roll.

It's okay to compare him to Jesus—but just try to compare him to Beethoven, Duke Ellington, or The Beatles. Then you'll know where you and your gramophone stand.

"I sure faked it for a long time," Elvis said of his guitar-playing at one of his final concerts. By then his self-pity was so obscenely thick, but it is sadness which brings me back to my favorite recordings and my best hopes. When I was 32 I moved to a northern city, largely to follow what I figured was a last chance at love. I still taught but only on a part-time basis, making ends meet with another part-time job I had with the Parks Commission. Even if I had the chance now to teach on a full-time basis I doubt I'd have the chops to pull it off.

"Fat Elvis becomes an emblem for the corrupt redneck quarters of unsophisticated America. From a publishing perspective, I don't think there's anything wrong with that vision, I have been an Elvis fan long enough to know how this vision of Elvis has wide currency. The middle-class audience I think shares this revulsion for the Fat Elvis trope and are usually glad to see their prejudices affirmed. Yet one of the reasons why Elvis is still so loved is how he remains welcoming to those poor folk whose tastes have not been defined by high-minded concepts like *University*."

If F. Scott Fitzgerald were alive today one of the things I'm sure he would say (besides "wow! flavored-vodka!") is that people without cable TV, *they are different from you and me.*

Hemingway Hero

The Hemingway Hero was a little bar in the most tourist-happy area of Apsicola Beach. It used be a dingy rub's tavern called The Quays; centered by a large teardrop-shaped bar and where, every Saturday, an out-of-tune band called Hazzard Country would play as the regulars slept along. Nowadays, they serve frozen drinks and have ladies night specials and, worst of all, the kind of lighting that assumes people are not ashamed of their splotchy faces.

Anyway, I was spending a lot of time at the Hemingway, trying to avoid my apartment where I had unplugged the phone. I was trying to get well away from my life at the English department at Southeast University where the term was coming to a close—it had been three days since I heard from a snooty colleague how one of my students, smarting from a D grade I gave him in Modern Fiction, was going around the department bragging he had "bought a gun with food stamps."

I don't think I took the threat seriously, but was weary at the sense of disgrace: a student who couldn't take their grade and say *fair enough!* brought me deep into longer dissatisfactions with my career choices. I liked "hiding out" and I liked creating scenarios that justified my refuge. The last place anybody who I knew would go to was a tourist beach bar—where Hemingway was merely a logo, a prototype for Jimmy Buffett. The Hero, despite its name, never even put sports on TV. The new owner scoured out the decades long stink of The Quays and wanted nothing to do with a sit-down chat bar. It was supposed to be young: good times, good fun, but the transition was uneasy.

The truth was, any student who could manage to throw in the part about "food stamps" probably knew more about modern fiction than I had given him credit for. When I first heard of the threat, I actually asked the department secretary if I should call the police. She advised me, like it happened all the time, that I should make some kind of official acknowledgment I had heard these noises. "That will help you in court in case he actually tries something," she said. "But don't worry, somebody has to tell these kids that they can't get away with it all of the time." The secretary was beloved for her uncharitable views of students and faculty alike.

So, as usual, I took it to the Hero, where chicken wings were called "wing dings" and where the oldest songs on the DJ's playlist were by U2. One night, as the ocean breeze was picking up the punishing humidity of the coming summer, I met this woman who looked about my age. She was red-haired and petite, and obviously just a nudge away from telling some beerhall sap her sad story. I was that sap through and through: I bought her a glass of wine and we got to talking about this and that. She was not a tourist and she too remembered The Quays—"I was hoping to get re-married there," she joked. I told her I was brought up in the farmlands of southern Minnesota "where everything's owned and operated by Green Giant Vegetables!" even though I only knew the suburbs of Minneapolis. "So what do you do here?" she asked and, when I told her I taught American fiction at the University, she smiled and said "way to go, Shakespeare; you still like girls though, right?"

She wasn't a college kid, and that was fine—I really didn't go after the coeds the way some of my colleagues would. The way I figured it, girls who'd sleep with their professors suffered from distinct ailments. I mean, a girl who would sleep with the young, hip poetry prof would probably suffer with low self-esteem issues; a girl who would sleep with the silver-haired philosopher would probably suffer from father issues; and a girl who would sleep with me would probably suffer from glaucoma.

By the time the guys in their basketball togs and the girls in their belly shirts were crowding the bar, we mumbled our geezery regrets and scrammed. We drove to her place way out in Coconut Strand. Her house, a 2-level seaside design in a gated community, certainly did not seem like the kind of place a single woman would buy. So, I joked "Where's your husband?" and she told me that he was in Kuwait City, part of a military police unit going in and out of Baghdad. If this disclosure was as embarrassing as my teaching at the University, I didn't say word one, but threw my coat on the MP's couch, happy to know this woman would not be looking for me to play house. *Good times, good fun.*

In the morning, I tiptoed through the house and through her husband's den. It was full of military effects: medals, citations, history books, show pistols and photographs. I half suspected that if I looked more diligently I'd find a picture autographed by a local Klansman. The pistols in particular brought me into the morning, the sweet shame of morning after regret: glad to have something else to run away from. That a student may be trying to kill me did not seem bothersome. It was the thought he may be on the side of justice which slowed me, made me go through the fridge to see if there was anything fancy I could snack on.

I waited for her to wake up to drive me back to the Hemingway where I left my car. I wanted to get back to my apartment and watch a TV show that would last until September.

"A D is a solid grade," I kept saying to myself. No questions asked. It wasn't nearly as questionable as the B-/C+ trap where profs usually fantasy-camped in the spring. In my dreams I'd see C+ students in tears, rejected from firms with strict "No C's" purviews, such nice kids and such a hardassed prof—would it have killed me to have raised their grades a little?. I'd see the B- students asleep in the cafeteria and when they'd wake, their faces creased by a book used as a pillow, they'd laugh about what a honeydew Modern Fiction is. Just faces and names, the same kids who came into the Hemingway and sang along to Nickelback. In my dreams, Disgruntled D stood there with an oil-black .357 pointed at my head. "What to make of a diminished thing," he'd scoff before drawing the hammer back.

In a sweat, I phoned the department and found Disgruntled D's address. The kid lived right in the heart of the city, where I imagined German tourists were popped on a regular basis. A hell of a neighborhood, but you can't get sandwiches like that in the suburbs—that kind of place.

I practically raced there, as if I was interceding in a hostage situation. He acted like he expected me, standing with a firm, aristocratic posture, like he had been up since dawn reading Dos Passos, wondering whose string quartets he would listen to when it was time for his fun. "I hear you're upset about your final grade?" I said.

"A D is a pass," he said softly; "or something like credit."

He asked me if I wanted coffee, or maybe some tea. He said he was working on a short story. "It's not really finished . . . would you like to see it?"

"I was hoping we could get this straightened out—you know you missed more than 50% of class, don't you?"

"Oh, I know," he said. "Why not just read the stupid story?"

I sat down and read, though it was very hard to settle down and get to the plot, what with thinking he'd be behind me like Robert De Niro with a baseball bat. The story was in the third person, lots of physical detail of city streets and hallways. A man named Fielder is in love with a sophomore named Connie. She is interested but only if nothing better comes along but she reluctantly agrees to go on a date with him to a *vernissage*. The weird modern paintings are described in exquisite detail. Images of translucent fish, poisonous nasturtiums, and mountains of ocelot bones. At the gallery, the daters bump into a senior who the sophomore is *really* interested in. They all leave together, get risqué drunk in a touchy jazz bar, go to Connie's room and stumble into a 3-way scene. The scene is handled with care: no coarse words, no diversion from the descriptive tone of the piece. Fielder, in the end, makes some acknowledgment of how horrible he was going to feel the next day, how weird-o it all was, but at the same time he just wanted to (yuk) "concentrate on loving his half" (double yuk).

"This is interesting," I said. "Have you ever thought of going into creative writing?"

"Drop dead!" he scoffed.

I knew he had the nerve to just scribble out his final exam, using the minimum amount of time, rarely referring to the modern fiction we studied, and once caustically trashing what he called "smile, smile, smile professors."

"I may just do that—they tell me you're making threats about a gun."

He laughed. "Are you for real? Is that what this is about, per-fessor? You're not here to give me the grade I deserve?"

"Somebody said you were threatening me."

"Maybe somebody—or maybe a few people—at the department is trying to make you look stupid."

"Well, I hardly need their help. Tell me then, what grade do you think you deserve?"

"I don't know," he said. "B- or C+. I don't know."

"Which one?"

"I don't know."

"Which one!"

"I don't know!" he screamed. I wanted to point a gun at his head and make him choose. But, I stood up in his apartment, a spare cubicle of off-white walls, bits of paper thumb-tacked everywhere. "I'll tell you what I'll do," I said, "because you've done such a good job presenting your case, I'm going to open the files and adjust your grade."

Claiming I made a clerical error, I gave the short story writer a B. What did it matter? All those students who accepted their C's as their just desserts—they're the ones who should have shot me.

Worse, I invited the young writer to hang out at the Hemingway with me and, one night, when the MP's wife came in, all dolled up, I leaned over and whispered into the kid's ear all the lurid details of my conquest.

Enlish 218
Poetry
(3 Credits)

Poetry: it not only lets you know The Raven quothe "nevermore," it helps you remember if the van's "a-rockin" maybe you shouldn't come "a-knockin." This course begins with one question: aside from offering a stage for grown men to wear big white blouses, what's the use of poetry in today's world? This course ends with the happier question "who wants cake?" We learn the basic diction of poetic analysis and how to not giggle when people say "diction." For example, "William Shatner" may sort of rhyme with "silly fat girl" but it's hardly a nice thing to say, so what would be a more effective way to slander Captain Kirk? Should all poems, in fact, be about Sulu? In this course you will also learn how show business attorneys never read poetry—so, please purchase the course-pack, Courtney Love's Plot to Kill P. Diddy, before classes start. Also required reading: Thoughts Poetical, Imaginative Airs and Whimsied Musings by Ignatius J. Hedgehog, Esq. We come to a solid understanding of how poetry is like homemade wine: people will say they like it, even raving "this is really good!" but they are lying. Nobody likes your homemade wine! Do you think anyone would serve that at a wedding? Students will be encouraged to read on their own, to work on their own, to be quiet in class and to not disturb the professor, who is busy writing a cookbook called Secrets of the Epstein-Barr Kitchen.

The Return of Grimace

Every year, it's guaranteed at least one ad in the TV rotation will stick in my head and start destroying brain cells previously wasted on mathematical theories and the specific dates of loved ones' birthdays. The dream is, one fine day, when my head is finally filled to capacity with jingles for local grouting firms, I will no longer have to bother with such trifles as novel-reading or pants-wearing.

I love shampoo ads, particularly their insistence on presenting these microscopic images where a single hair looks like a suspension bridge cable. I could watch those ads forever. I don't know what pH is but I do know it's supposed to be balanced. But, not so long ago, as I was considering employment opportunities in the vast food service industry myself, I was greatly disturbed by a new set of McDonald's ads. These ads—featuring celebrities like the strangely rehabilitated Donald Trump and *Barbershop 2* star Cedric The Entertainer (and isn't "Cedric" a rather pompous name for Mrs. The Entertainer to have given her son?)—were meant to promote the questionable "McExtra" burger.

While it's hard to describe the McExtra without resorting to phrases like "colo-rectal roulette" it's basically a quarter pounder with lettuce and tomato—a McDLT without the spectacular *hotside-hot/coolside-cool* technology. In other words: delicious! How people can go two meals in a row without having a McExtra is to me a miracle as profound as walking on water or the 99 cent margarita.

In some ways, it's amazing that I can recall the McExtra ad. I can understand why I keep "forgetting" my *Ft. Lauderdale Rump Shaker* T-shirt is not appropriate for a job interview, but I don't know why I can only seem to remember one or two ads at any time. One always being that old ad where Punchy, the Hawaiian Punch mascot, smacks the crap out of some doddering old tourist who could not understand the delightful *double-entendre* "How would you like a nice Hawaiian Punch?" I feel more like that doddering tourist as time goes on. People are always saying "Hey have you seen that Andy Griffith ad, where he's singing 'The Wreck of The Edmund Fitzgerald'?" and I'm always going, "No, I don't recall" as if I'm on the witness stand for a capital crime.

Anyways, what was really weird about these McExtra ads was the celebs were having a detailed discussion about the McExtra with the McDonaldland character Grimace. You know, Grimace, the big purple thing with the googly eyes that loves McDonald's shakes. *Grimace!* This is what really disturbs me. It was my understanding Grimace was *strictly* a milkshakes character! Not burgers or fries, just shakes.

Just shakes.

-Why is Grimace, of all McDonaldlanders, being consulted about developments in burgers?

-What would Grimace know about a hamburger?

Grimace's monomaniacal obsession with McDonald's shakes is the whole basis of his personality. Did that purple freak go to some drastic McDonaldland re-education center just so he could talk about burgers with The Donald? "Grimace, sweetheart, it's like I don't know who you are anymore."

Asking Grimace about burgers strikes me as a completely pointless exercise, like asking your gym teacher "Why do I have to take off my shorts?" or like asking "How's the seafood?" when walking into Denny's. Can Grimace even talk? He doesn't say anything in the ads, not even a stray comment to Trump like "Nice hair."

Just *what* is Grimace?

Some kind of shake-loving, upright purple cow?

A draped-in-velvet manatee?

When you think about it zoologically, Grimace is clearly related to the same species as *Sesame Street*'s Cookie Monster. Both have similar body shapes—dark colors, mottled hides, those darting black eyes and, most significantly, both have an obsessive compulsion to consume one single item of American junk food. They're practically twins. Of course—and this is crucial—Grimace is less of a moralist about the whole thing. Unlike Cookie Monster, Grimace doesn't care if you can count from one to ten, he just wants his milkshake. "Ya, ya, C is for

Cookie; J is for Just give me my fucking shake, okay?"

It makes you wonder about his name, though. "Grimace" is so sad sounding. "Aw, Grimace, why the grimace?" I wonder if Grimace's roots can be traced back to the old country where he was known as "Grim-a-chay," and where his ancient mule-training and cheese-making skills were lost in the bizarre flux of Modern America? And maybe his love of shakes and his newly anglicized name are desperate attempts to assimilate in the social strata of McDonaldland, where happiness is not just a pursuable right but a pretty darn tasty meal. Maybe in the old country *Señor Grimace* used to eat something less middle American—like rice, or children.

After all there is a carefully delineated *McDonaldland ethnic hierarchy* which is more rigid than the Indian caste system or the Elizabethan "Great Chain of Being." If we look at the chain of command:

Ronald McDonald
Mayor McCheese
Big Mac
Birdy
Grimace
Hamburglar
The French Fry Guys

we see, clearly, a Scotsman was in charge (Ronald), which could mean McDonaldland's like a Canadian bank, whereas the silly, hiccupping Mayor McCheese and the billy-club twirling "Big Mac" represented the corrupt Irish muscle of old power—the Tammany Hall of McDonaldland. Ronald leaned on his Irish precincts to shore up his unchallenged power as the de facto leader of McDonaldland. Of course, a franchise as devoted to public support as McDonald's knows, you have to shore up the support of potato-lovers in order to rule. Or, as a recent potential employer said to me, "The problem with democracy is you have to let the Irish vote."

I wonder, whatever happened to Big Mac? Was he whacked by Hamburglar the way Michael Corleone whacked Captain McClusky? Perhaps Hamburglar's long absence means he's been away for something much more serious than burger theft. Hamburglar, what with his strange ethnic phrasings ("robblerobble"), is perhaps a cautionary tale about what happens if you don't respect the law of the new world when accommodating one's freakish obsession with McDonald's food. When the guy in the documentary *Super Size Me* made his gonzo critique of American fast food by eating only Mickey D's cuisine, I thought the parable of the Hamburglar should have been invoked, suggesting that while McDonaldland may have been less focused on the needs for a low fat diet, it does indeed think fixating on its products can lead to strange moral problems.

Apparently, "McDonaldland" was created by the ad agency of Needham, Harper & Steers in the early '70s and Grimace began his life as "The Evil Grimace"—a six-armed monster who terrorized McDonaldland by *stealing* milkshakes. Just like the morally uncontained Hamburglar steals hamburgers. But somewhere along the way, Grimace had an epiphany and decided to try to fit in, while Hamburglar went the way of Dillinger. Grimace stopped stealing shakes, and drastically had four of his six arms amputated—much like Marie Osmond did in the late '80s. Some people will do anything to fit into America. After all, even the orginal McDonald's mascot, the winking, burger-faced Speedee no longer holes up in McDonaldland. Could Speedee be the victim of a botched suicide pact with Speedy, the Alka-Seltzer kid?

Perhaps less in need of a radical make over is, to slightly mix metaphors, the poultry-product hawker Birdy. Not an original citizen of McDonaldland, Birdy is an adorable little chicken with braided pig tails and aviator's glasses, who not only heralds the introduction of tasty poultry items to the menu, but brings a little touch of femininity to the boys' club atmosphere of McDonaldland. Of course, I don't know why one assumes a walking, talking hamburger is male, but without the tell-tale signs of mascot sexual differentiation (big eyelashes, a pink bow) the process of discrimination known as "The Ms. Pacman Standard" is still in place. In other words, please don't tell me Happy Foot, the McGregor sock mascot, is really a woman because then I'd have to embark on a long, painful re-examination of my relationship to the strongest male role model in my life. Birdy, however, introduces a more significant problem to Hamburger Valley. Where Mayor McCheese and Big Mac are not cows, but humanoid-processed food products,

Birdy is an actual chicken, the living thing which is turned into a McNugget. Yet, like a violin-playing pig outside a Southern barbecue, she promotes the consumption of her own kind. Though it is possible to see the transformation of chicken to McNugget in religious terms, the McNugget being a more enlightened reincarnation, Birdy's endorsement of auto-cannibalism is still very disturbing—sort of like hearing Secretariat saying steak "chevaline" is better than a rib eye. Luckily for her, Birdy is now keeping a low profile, and the little McNugget characters are nowhere to be seen in this go go era of the Golden Arches.

Things haven't been as great in McDonaldland since Ronald's Saturday morning glory days. Maybe the company, busy trying to promote pizzas and boneless rib sandwiches, has had less time to celebrate the citizens of its own mythic land. I wonder if the French Fry Guys still declaim their perfect collective harmony since they've become the Freedom Fry Guys? In the past, the French Fry Guys resisted cherished notions of American individualism: there was no French Fry Guy more important than the next, no singular French Fry Guy—no wonder they're all so cozy in a RED carton! The jig is up, *Comrade* French Fry Guy.

Who knows if Trump is planning on telling Grimace "You're fired" as McDonald's heads into a more uncertain, more Justin Timberlake-heavy, future. Grimace, perhaps another casualty of the dot com drop, may have grudgingly come back to the work force of the current McDonaldland administration—much like Jimmy Carter. In a show of loyalty, Grimace may have to hold a "shamrock shake" high and toast the leadership of Big Mac and Mayor McCheese. Grimace would say nothing, he is mute, but he may be thinking "Once, the children of the world wept for the absence of green Saint Patrick's day imitation milkshakes but now there is no crying—for we are all together again in McDonaldland."

Were only such opportunities available to the inarticulate and ice cream loving citizens outside of McDonaldland. May McDonaldland long thrive—even as it will, in the future, come up with new challenging characters: the prosecutorial *District Attorney McPork* who sues people with the same passion of a crazed moron in the drive-thru and, of course, get ready to say hello to *Salad Stevie, The Most Sensitive Boy in McDonaldland*. Poor Salad Stevie: like me, he has a long way to go.

from *The Secret Correspondence between Fonzie's Jacket and Christina Aguilera*

To: Fonzie's Jacket
c/o The Smithsonian Institute
National Museum of American History
Washington, DC

From: Christina Aguilera
c/o RCA Records
New York, NY

Dear Fonzie's Jacket,

I don't know if you know me or if you read the tabloids (but if you do,
please don't believe them when they say I'm like this huge skank who's
done it with all the Los Angeles Clippers) but I just started watching
episodes of *Happy Days* and was really digging your work when somebody told me you were at the Smithsonian, along with other items of
TV apparel. Dr. Huxtable's sweaters, Alex P. Keaton's knit ties, Rhoda's
scarves, who knows—maybe one day one of the thongs I've worn at the
MTV Music Awards will be there with you!

Anyway, Jacket, hope you're having a nice time where you are—
you're awesome! Do you ever hear from The Blue Windbreaker—that's
such a funny name, like he's a sad guy who farts all the time. What
shows do you watch there?

Your fan,

Christina

Dear Christina,

Thanks for writing to me. Things get slow and dull around here what with Urkel's Suspenders acting so high & mighty all the time, I don't expect much mail. So, naturally, I was touched to have received a letter from someone I admire so much. You make Kelly Clarkson sound like a lawn mower and you make Britney Spears sound like Dick Vitale. I defend you all the time. Archie Bunker's Chair is always going on about how your song "Beautiful" is contradictory: he says if the singer is saying "Words can't bring me down" why does she, in the end of the song, say "So, don't you bring me down today"? Isn't that contradictory? I swear, Archie Bunker's Chair is worse than Archie Bunker!

The Blue Windbreaker is such a loser, whimpering around here about how I took his spotlight and all that Salieri bullshit. But I guess you're used to that what with you, Justin and Britney all coming from the same Mouseketeer club—jeez, what kind of adrenaline did they line the sandboxes with there? Really, I see kids here all the time and it seems to me the best they can do is to not eat the paper found on the floor and here's the three of you—all huge stars!

I won't ask you about the real story between you and Brit—I think we all understand the fickleness of the business and the importance of true talent.

Nobody wants Potsie's Pants.

Your friend,
Fo-Jay

Dear Fo-Jay,

Thanks for defending "Beautiful" and not busting me about Britty's kissy thing—being asked about that girl every day of my life is a stinker. Maybe that's our genius: the English have Shakespeare, the Russians have *War & Peace* and we have *From Flab to Rad—Plastic Surgery Secrets of the Stars*. Sometimes I envy the lives I read about in fan mail: the basketball tournaments, the quiet small town intersection, the convenience store's bulletin board, watching people come and go—the deliberate manner of those who have real lives at home.

Anyways, I've been on the road and my voice feels as stretched out as Jared's old pants. Ha! I admire the people who've done this for a long time: Aretha Franklin, Willie Nelson, Lyle Waggoner. Hard to imagine I'll be singing "Dirrrty" when I'm 60 years old but, you know, I really hope I do. Peggy Lee must have sung "Fever" until she was 104.

You never responded to me when I asked what you watched on TV? You're not one of these "I don't even *own* a TV" nimrods who think they've solved the code of the Rosetta Stone are you?

Big ups,

Xina

Chère Xina,

No! I have seen the Hope Diamond and the Spirit of St. Louis in person but I am not that type. I'm thrilled you asked me what I watch today as everyone figures I would only know *Happy Days, Laverne and Shirley* and, maybe, *Mork and Mindy*. But I watch more now—in the late night darks of the Smithy I do keep up with what's on and, in the morning, I say this little prayer:

Time to watch the sun kiss the sky
Time to watch Dr. Phil make the fat people cry

I actually had a dream where Dr. Phil kept yelling at a pork chop that was sitting in his chair. I also like that *Average Joe* series—it's like a live action version of *Carrie* where they get some good looking guy to take Carrie to the prom and the spot where the blood will be dumped on her. It's the same thing, the model/actress gets some schmuck to fall in love with her (and how could he not, he's as dopey-looking as a mule in a top hat) and then she dumps him for the hunky model/actor. I feel sorry for the models actually: they didn't invent the *Average Joe* hypocrises they are forced to live out. Who wants to go out with Ol' Ugly? I miss the sitcom *Emeril*—that was amazing. I could have stared at that thing for months and would have never understood just what it was I was watching.

I understand what you mean about the life outside—wanting to just be a jacket on some lovable dope going through a mid-life crisis. But, it is better to be who you are, to know that God has blessed you— much like he blessed Burt Reynold's wig and Shaquille O'Neal's shoe.

-Fo-Jay

P.S. I'm so pleased you mentioned Lyle Waggoner. Did you notice he was left off the marquee for recent promotions for a DVD edition of *The Carol Burnett Show*? That's like making a documentary on wood-boring pests and forgetting the termite.

Hey Fo-Jay,

Those reality series are so cruel—and I see what you mean about feeling blessed. It's just a fantasy—to be relieved of the anxiety that informs one's reality. You know, in this business you're always responding to some bell or whistle—often you're treated as if you were sitting on a bench by the exit of a Tijuana bar. None of us are any better than the *Average Joe* heartbreakers. Of course, the woman working at Pizza Hut to feed her family has it much harder than you or I, but sometimes I can't help but wonder what it's like to live a "real" life; to not have one's sexuality microscoped in the press, to know that people think you're special even though you don't have a lot of cash?

The occasional free slice would be nice, sure, but what could be worse than slogging it out for tips at the Hut? Working at Hooters? Working at a Hooters in Hallandale, Florida? Can you imagine the stuff you'd have to hear come out of customers' mouths? I'd imagine being asked what the dumbest thing you've heard in Hooter's is sort of like being asked what's the most insufferable episode of *Reba* or what's the most pretentious song on a Tom Waits album? I imagine everyday you get somebody coming in asking "What's in the chicken wings?" or "What would you recommend for someone on a diet?" I bet you not one of those nice girls in the little orange shorts says "I don't know, Jumbo, a .44?"

I know I am grateful because I know I am no better than anyone. God bless.

Love, Xina

P.S. What's the deal with the opening montage in *Fresh Prince of Bel Air*? Does Will take a cab all the way from Philadelphia? Do you find Will a little snobby about the poor cab driver?

Dear Xy,

Thanks for your letter and I understand what you mean about wanting something you've declared "normal." My heart is nothing if not a sleeve (sorry) that says "jealous of the Cunninghams."

I am here forever so, naturally, I'm jealous of how you get to travel everywhere. I want to say: What's the Sbarro's like in Tiananmen Square? What do you talk about if children don't even know who won *Survivor* or if they don't even seem to fear Michael Jackson? What kind of American music seems particularly awful when you're in the grips of a funk far away from home?

As for the *Prince*, one might assume Will takes the cab all the way from Philly to LA, and the "rare" smell he seeks to escape is his own cross-country stink. However, in the first ep. there's an extended version of the rap where The Prince flies first class to LAX. Something about rhyming *champagne* with *plane*. You're right that Will's diss indicates his quick endorsement of the show's episodic class narrative: that, like Eliza Doolittle, he has a deep down "class" which proves worthy of being distinguished from other playground thugs and from immigrant cab drivers. By about episode 6, Will stops wearing that stupid hat and that's how he warmed Mr. Sheffield's heart and became The Nanny. What remains strange is that Judge Banks did not send a car: spotting a yellow cab in Bel Air is reason enough for groundskeepers to break out the shot guns.

F-jay

FJ,

Travel and escape were still on my mind as I found myself in Albany, NY, recently and was watching a documentary about a man who made a theme park in the Adirondack Mountains called "The Land of Make-Believe." "The Land of Make-Believe" was, apparently, really popular in the '60s—well before theme parks were a worn part of the American crossroads. Anyways, the gimmick of this place was everything was scaled to kid-size: saloons, banks, churches, castles—all fitted to the kiddies so they could experience the joy an adult feels when he or she would line up in a bank to deposit a check. Anyways, a heavy spring flooding of the Ausable River wiped out "The Land of Make-Believe" in 1979. Nowadays, the old creator just wanders around the remains of his empire, thinking of how he'll pay his debts before he dies. *Half-scale craps tables don't come for free.* So goes all make-believes, I thought, watching that guy. It was sad but it was the sadness that I know will one day be mine: when they don't buy my records anymore, when they don't ask me to appear on shows anymore—not even *Dame Edna.*

When far away from home and I feel blue, believe me, it's the absence of American music which brings you further down. I would do anything to hear some cornball whopper like "The Man in the Mirror" or "The Fishing Song" and not find myself among Euro-cool nimrods listening to Die Technischehausen's *Robotspiel.* The whole freaking world is on this crazed anti-American thing, FJ, scapegoating us for every single fault of theirs. The way people talk to me—the palpable anger in their voices—"How do you answer for your cowboy country's role in the conspiracy to make us drink wine made from your fried chicken?"—it's like I personally gave birth to Donald Rumsfeld.

Sorry I'm all over the place. Hey, do you ever get afraid?

Love, X

O X,

Thanks for your letter I know you're busy and I won't get to hear from you as much when you're on the road. Do you remember that episode of *The Brady Bunch* where Greg becomes singing sensation "Johnny Bravo?" It's so good: Greg gets a big head and starts acting like a twitty superstar but soon enough he learns he got the gig not because he could sing but because he fit the studio's Johnny Bravo outfit. You see, the Johnny Bravo outfit is the star—not the voice and certainly "not the soul that is inside" (to quote your rival, Avril Lavigne). This is the way it is everywhere, hi or lo, and whether it's a rocker's leather bracelet or the writer's back-jacket photo in a turtleneck—the gestures of identity are as small and as predictable as the Hooters girls' outfit.

I live quietly, more like that guy in your ghost theme park than the prostitute in the Tijuana bar. I always tried to mask my fears—would do anything to pretend I did not notice people in the crowd laughing at me. They call me *Fonzie* or, worse, *Winkler* and I am never perceived as myself but as a very small colony—a comment on someone else's power. It takes a lot of poison to try to tame something as wriggly as one's fears. Wild nights: Corey Feldman's leather jacket, the one with the punk studs on the shoulder and Corey Haim's leather jacket, the one with the deep, secret pockets. There were such hard times in the past. When I'd read about how it was over for me, I admit the small-bite clamor of those notes destroyed me—made me think of a dark, quiet closet—and I learned how to not want for actual company, to say no to invitations, to dread the kind of summer light where people can see you—tatters and all. But, no matter, I'm still here and, to be honest, I didn't learn much in those days when I would not stop killing myself. I'm still here!

Sweet love! FJ

The Gospel According to St. Matthew Introduced by Batman

All things are delivered unto me of my Father: and no man knoweth the
Son, but the Father 11:27

My father was killed by a street bandit in a scuffle over my mother's
pearls.   You have heard it all before. *"This will shut you up, BLAM!"*
Thirty years later, I tracked a subway vigilante to his hideaway and,
when I had my hands at his lapels, he confided in me, as if we were in
the middle of a long campaign, drunk in a bivouac. He said: "When I
told my father that I couldn't work at his restaurant any more because
I wanted to go to school I might as well have stuck a knife in him."
Then, the subway vigilante let his body go limp and finished his tale:
"Two years later, my father was shot behind his restaurant's cash regis-
ter." I did not go *O my brother* and let him slip back into the shadows
of Gotham's abandoned factories. I took him in and, soon enough, I
was telling the district attorney, over scotch, "Anything I can do to help,
just call."

Come unto me, all ye that labor 11:28

In Wayne Manor we did not sit around comparing cuff links. The man
with the wings, the detective among gospel-writers, the proof-setter, the
point-maker: Matthew's theosophy is hard for me to gather into one
brief introduction. How could I not suspect crabbed reaction to anything I might say: i.e. "Easy for you, Mr. Moneybags." I asked my but-
ler Alfred, as he was setting down a bowl of Manhattan clam chowder
in front of the batcomputer, what he thought of the first gospel writer
and he chimed "Did you miss your matins, Master Bruce?"   But that's

Alfred, too sweet to challenge me, too faithful to wonder what's really on the other side of the batcave. On my own, I try my best to haunt the greystone taverns and girlie shows: the places where hard workers blend in with my parents' killers. Blue-collar crude mauler molly-mother muddy winter weather elbows all the time. "Criminals are superstitious" I have said in the comfort of my grand library and all the pinewood benches and warped stools and *heyas* and *whaddyasays* accumulate and before I die I swear I'll find the joker who made my laughing matters such a stocking foot in my mouth.

the heavens were opened unto him, and he saw the Spirit of God descending like a dove 3:16

No matter how hard I punch his face, he can't help himself. No matter how severely I break his legs, he's still gonna teach me *The Electric Slide*. The Joker's confession: "Jesus takes me to the Mall, like he's my Grampa or something. He doesn't know that I've been there a million times. He doesn't know that once, when I was fourteen, I slept in the furniture department and told my Mom I had stayed over at Rob McLennan's. He doesn't know about the fire I set in the stairwell, the coat-stealing scam, the daily lunch of strawberry donuts at a stand called Lucky Thirteen. What a maroon! Jesus stops at Starbucks, tired of looking at basketball shoes, and tells me about how Abraham Lincoln's uncles called him lazy because he wanted to study on his law books instead of going to hunt snakes from the farmstead. That's like me, I thought; except I shirked my snake-killing duties more out of wanting to smoke pot and watch reruns of *Get Smart*. Thank you, Jesus."

if it be possible, let this cup pass from me 26:39

Matthew, ever the riddle-wit, connects the dots and I swear it is the most meaningful chicken sandwich I have ever had. I have skimmed his great book at least twice. His man could set the poplar trees on fire, and the fire of the poplars could replace the traffic lights, and the happy motorists would see JC, not as big a hippie as you might think, ride bombs like a fat rich kid on a pony. Take me back to the handgun kick-back, take me back to the streets of Lebanon, Tennessee where it may be answered, "If Jesus were alive today, what kind of assault weapon would he use?" No superhero popinjay, I am Batman, scientist. Anyway, when The Big Hippie was in Gethsemane predicting his own death, a mysterious light appeared in the sky. "Did you see that?" Peter asked the two sons of Zebedee. They said they thought it was some kind of beast, or beast-like thing, a cranky marmot at the very least, but an altogether bad omen of bad things—an embarrassing omen that, like your girlfriend, talks too loud after a few drinks. "I have come for thee. I am setting up in thine parlor, drinking thine fine port. I am especially drinking thine fine port."

Are not two sparrows sold for a penny? Yet not one of them will fall to the ground apart from the will of your Father. And even the very hairs of your head are all numbered. So don't be afraid 10: 29-31

The infamous pianist Chandell (a.k.a. Fingers) was giving a "command performance" for President Nixon at the White House. You could see from Trisha Nixon's face that everybody was loving it. However, Chandell was actually using a player piano during his performance, a secret which his own twin brother tried to blackmail him with. In need of quick money, Chandell wanted to marry Aunt Harriet but thought he stood a better chance with her if Bruce Wayne (me) and Dick Grayson (my ward) were out of the way first. I swear, the man tried to turn us into a player piano roll! He was all business, tying us down, readying us to be pulped, papered, and pressed into a roll that plays "Music Box Dancer." And, for awhile, I didn't know what to do, I was just lying there, sweating under my cowl, thinking about women with great, great hair. For the love of Wella Balsam, God has been stringent in matters of hair, can we not allow the followers of Jesus Christ to follow advances in bouncy, streak-free, wholesome manageability? Where does "Thou canst not make one hair white or black" (5:36) fit in with *100 Great New Styles for Around the Office*? Read closely and, apparently, there are things more profound than a blonde reporter who'll get in your car just because you look rich. I have escaped Chandell's trap but I am going to die. Vicki Vale, in chemotherapy, takes great comfort in Matthew 10:29; Aquaman, who's gone a little thin up top, is more defensive.

And, finally, Batgirl does her thing. What a dork, sitting against a coffee bar, writing her first French 101 essay on her inexplicable admiration for Liza Minnelli. *Avec ses yeux brilliants. . .* But she was something else standing on her head on her batcycle firing off a full clip from her Bat-Glock 9. In another part of town, I reminded Catwoman that a beauty as rare as hers did not deserve somebody as hurried as I was. Forgive my impatience as I head to the southlands. Kitty Kat is sitting in the kitchen just afterwards, acting like she's interested in something in the newspaper. I ask Catwoman right there if she ever thought of Jesus? "Do you mean as a sexual partner?" she said without skipping a beat. Has it come to this? The Nazarene's Sacred Thing? The King of Kings' Ding-a-Ling? Emmanuel's One-Eyed Whale? The Redeemer's Wiener? The Rock's Cock? The Son of God's Holy Rod? The Man from Galilee's Pet Monkey? The Holy Son's Love Gun? The Big Enchilada's Big Enchilada? The Paschal Lamb's Battering Ram? The Anointed One's Great Big One? And I'm thinking about Batgirl again, walking by the place where she works by day, just a little coffee shop, the cute girl who works in the coffee shop, the cutest of coffees for me, me first please.

Bosola

Yesterday, I cut off my ear and sent it to Cher. It wasn't the cutting off part that was hard. The knife my old girlfriend gave me for my twenty-fifth birthday was scalpel sharp and handy. It was the sending it to Cher part that was hard. Licking the envelope, checking the zip code, a towel tied around my head—but not too tight. Blood darker than what I've seen before (i.e. the watercolor stuff from wrists in 1985, addicted to cocaine, stuck in a small town). Dizzy, staggering through the hot streets, dropping it in the mailbox, giving a little valediction into the tin box as it set forth on its odyssey. With my good ear I could hear a pleasant echo.

I could imagine Cher's face upon opening my delicate offering, and seeing that fresh pink bloom, so small, so small.

Yesterday in Texas the Governor was bragging about how tough he was on crime. He was gladhanding at a barbecue in Corpus Christi, standing under the blue sky, his hair crabbed in a Gulf wind. He said "My government is committed to convicting and quickly executing the murderers in this state." It's been a very dry spring, everybody is on edge, despairing of another brutal summer. Nobody much believes, or cares, about reports of a rejuvenation in the oil fields due to a new computer technique for risk-free drilling. One day the whole state will be a vast Sahara with two hundred-foot-high dunes just outside of Houston. I will leave my plans to build some kind of pyramid in this wasteland.

My name is Bosola and these are the things I do for fun. Once I worked for a man who collected debts the classic way: snipping off body parts of the indebted. Oh, they weren't just poor drug addicts and thieves, but thieves of a "respect" which my boss would say was worth more than "all the gold in Goldenton."

I didn't think much about Cher then: but now I have it all down. Here are some bones: marriage to Sonny, "I Got You Babe," the TV show, Chastity, the Bob Mackie outfits, divorce from Sonny, Greg Allman and Elijah Blue, obscurity and restitution by Bob Altman, then other movies, an academy award, called David Letterman an asshole, "Do You Believe in Life After Love?"

I prefer whiskey that has chunky sediment and at night I see goblins, standard size, breezing around the ceiling. They must speak Romanian. In the future we will all speak the same language, we will all have perfect bodies, every time we have sex it will be a wonderful life-affirming experience and only American Express card members will be allowed to live.

This morning the doctor told me that I didn't damage everything in that ear and that I should retain some level of hearing. Plastic surgery is a definite option. But he would have to see when the infection subsided. The side of my head was a bit of a mess. The doctor's hopefulness made me worry my Van Gogh's ear was less than perfect, and Cher would think it was some dried apple skin and would have her thugs throw it out.

Like me, Cher is fascinated by ancient Egypt. Before she was so ultra-conscious of her media image (or less manic about controlling that image) she would tell anybody who would listen that she was Cleopatra in a previous life. "I WAS CLEOPATRA IN A PREVIOUS LIFE—CHER," *The National Examiner*, April 2, 1975. Her mansion, in the impenetrable parts of Bel Air, is a trove of ancient treasures worth millions. Sometimes she has her thugs dress as Egyptian footmen to amuse herself. Sometimes she bathes in rose-perfumed 2% milk and has self-professed cunnilingual-expert, bass-player, KISS member Gene Simmons play Anthony to her misunderstood Queen. I am hoping she'll put my ear in the jewelry box she bought at Sotheby's last fall: gold, ivory and lapis lazuli, another representation of Ti watching the hippopotamus hunt. Approximately 2212 B.C.

She has enough Egyptian style jewelry to merit her own pyramid. I don't want her to be jealous anymore of the formerly wasp-waisted Liz Taylor who played the Serpent O' the Nile in 1963. So jealous, *ma cherie*. And when global warming does turn this part of the confederacy into a lifeless desert, every Texan, black, white, hispanic, could band together to construct great pyramids to Cher, following the sanded-over road between El Paso and Beaumont. (Cher's face on a Sphynx in Ozona?)

Of course I've been to El Paso. I stayed in a Journey's End Motel that approached the river and I was always around drugs then, always around drug-money. I was visiting Juarez, seeking out a deal on a gold mask of one of the daughters of Akhenaten. The man who tried to sell it to me (it was a fake) was a "doctor" who specialized in laetrile treatments for desperate, rich Americans. At night, in the motel, I took some stuff I bought at the farmacia, and bounced about the city square, thinking of the river curling upwards into America.

This morning my doctor said what worried him was that I had lost a lot of blood. It wasn't all as neat as I pretend—I have to stay here in the hospital until I stop feeling dizzy, stop seeing goblins drooling onto the hospital floor. "Wipe that up, it's infectious," I say to the nurses. Dr. Suarez is a bit of a wuss, I told him I didn't care much about this and he got all puffy and upset. I think he slapped me. He said that if I was in trouble with bad people that I should tell the police "before animals like that get somebody who *does* care." So I told him "I didn't say I didn't care, I said I sent it to Cher!" My name is Bosola and Cher is Cher no matter what heaven the mayor of Palm Springs frequents. Dr. Suarez says she is meaningless. She is singing (or will) of the misery of those who are born great. Besides, I know somebody who was in with some bad people for a large amount. He went away for a year and now he has a nice home in the suburbs.

Cher will never love me, but she may appreciate the gesture. If love was at stake, cutting off my ear would be stupid. Sex is out of the question. What I've done isn't evil, like snipping off junkies' toes because they owe old Bosola money for blow. Cher will know now that I am out there, somewhere in Texas, following her career with a slave's eye. Maybe she would like an eye? She has a tattoo of a pharoah's eye on the northwest quad of her right ass-cheek. It is one of those slim pharoah-boys who died very young.

Yesterday I was in a totally different frame of mind. I haven't always done things like this: once, in Galveston, I thought of taking it all out to the ocean, but it was just a thought. Yesterday something happened. Maybe it had to do with the half-gallon vodka decanter, maybe I was lonely for my girlfriend who was smart enough to buy a knife.

I will eat butter, cheese, tropical oil, and cream tonight. I guess it isn't right. My name is Bosola and the rest is suicide poetry: you take a lobster in your hand, its pincers/claws filled with cyanide and in his delectable tail every stupid thing you ever said. And munch and chew and slurp and there all the anger is gone, slump to St. Ann, to an old lover, I don't care, I'm just tired of holding her captive, tired of asking her to shut up. Red claws everywhere: the mouth takes it and spews life out sick. I can't hear and here, as promised, the bitters are sauced: butter, cheese, tropical oil and cream. Thickened, the quiver in my voice will be gone. My name is Bosola, I am your creature.

Yesterday I cut off my ear and sent it to Cher.

Christmas Lake

Christmas was always a drag around Mrs. V.'s house what with her son living in the lake thinking *kill, kill,* and the December winds filling her living room. She was always eating soup, always talking about pink insulation.

I had been going there for her annual Christmas party since 1979 when we both were working at an office at the Department of Education in Albany. Mrs. V. was quite popular around the coffee service or photocopy machine; always cheerful, always full of interesting practical advice. "Just use a little club soda!" or "A winter scarf is perfect for your sister!" I can still hear her say. But sometime after the election of Ronald Reagan, she left the Department to tend to problems at her home up in the Adirondacks. They say the tragedy of her son Jamie would be immortalized in the fictional slasher films of the 1980s—but my knowledge of Jamie was vague; all I've heard is that her boy "sort of drowned."

Mrs. V. kept in touch with me, even after my divorce. She set great store in her Christmas party and even though I never had a good time, I found it hard to say no. She said she was preparing a special soup: "cauliflower carrot dill."

On the frozen surface of Chrysler Lake, I stood with Mrs. V. as she lowered Christmas nut-cakes into a hole in the ice. They would noiselessly recede into the cold water and in a minute or so, a burp-like bubble would emerge and echo into the far trees. Once all the nut-cakes were gone we went back to the house. "Christmas," she sighed. "What can you tell me about pink fiberglass insulation?"

Welcoming guests, ladling eggnog, singing along to Sammy Davis Jr.'s "Christmas Time All Over the World," offering advice on turkey-basting,

Mrs. V. was the model of affability. She did not care about *The New Yorker* or who was knocking boots in Hollywood. Personally, I had no idea what to talk about. It seemed strange to me that there were no other notable flavors of "nog" besides egg. What of bread nog? Or duck nog?

Ultimately there were about 25 people at the party, mostly yokels, most unfriendly. Some played cards. A guy who used to work with us before he moved to D.C. also showed up. He was in poor spirits. He had cancer and was to spend the holidays undergoing treatment. What was he doing out here? "I feel fine," he said. "That's the funny thing." Throughout the time he was in the house, he played along. He said to me: "It was nice of you to come—she hasn't been the same since her boy . . . well, you know."

At 2 p.m. we all sat down for her special soup. It tasted like rust. There was also a pork loaf, European crackers, a kind of wine, dry shrimp and jelly. After the food most of the guests found a way to excuse themselves. I found it too difficult to fabricate an excuse, and wavered in between the fantasy of "I have work to do" and the more honest but slightly insulting "I don't feel so good." Keeping with a trend I carefully worked on all my life, I did nothing.

Those who remained, sat in the living room, trying to stay warm, ready to be entertained. Mrs. V.'s lover, Eddie Peterson, brought by his pet monkey and they did a routine about tax-collecting. It was quite funny. The monkey yawned and yawned. The monkey's name was *Stephanini*. I ate more, drank more thick Christmas stuff and felt wide. I must have dozed off. I have a faint recollection of a vermouthy drink Eddie made called "The Dylan Thomas."

Once again I was standing on the frozen surface of Chrysler Lake. Eddie Peterson shot a hole in the ice with an automatic shot-gun. Mrs. V. stood bemused, hands in pockets, her false teeth a little loose in her mouth. "More nut-cake?" I asked, when Eddie suddenly came down hard with a rifle butt to the back of my shoulder, forcing me down, face first, into the snow and ice. He came down with two more blows, again to the general back area.

He grabbed me by the hair and smashed my face into the ice. Then he pulled me over to the hole and started dunking my head in the chunky ice-water. "Christmas cheer!" he said each time he put my head in. "Christmas cheer! Christmas cheer!"

Before I could feel ice water puddling in the small of my back, before I could taste blood from my mouth and nose, before my hair froze into dreadlocks, I swear I could hear that kid going *kill, kill*, thrashing about and going for my head like a snapping turtle.

When I stood up, I paused to focus on the vista of the other side of Chrysler Lake. There was nothing there that did not have the quality of gray.

Mrs. V. said to me, "We should get you some more soup for that cold of yours." Blood hardened and cracked on my face, flaking off and spotting the snow like pepper. I walked straight to my car and drove back to Albany.

Epilogue

I wanted to work throughout the holidays and put the incident behind me. I was good at that kind of thing. I bought everybody *K-Tel Pattystackers* as gifts, but did not share any desire to take time off to celebrate. I was fired on the day of the office party. I was typing up forms when my boss came up to me, drunk, and asked, "Do you like your job?"

I said, "Fry me for my crimes, shitface."

I didn't blame any of the events on Mrs. V. or Eddie Peterson or even my boss. I foolishly blamed it on Christmas itself, thinking the day's purpose was to emphasize the birth into sin, to slyly assure death is obvious in every pine needle—so, screw everybody because it's mine, mine, mine. Like a friend who treats you shabbily once, you forget all the good stuff. For a bit, I pretended it was like that all along.

A few years after my post in Albany was attrited, a *New York Post* headline screamed "SUMMER SLAYFEST IN LAKE CO." Mrs. V. had died.

Now, I am a sucker for the Christmas lights on the convenience stores on the off-ramps of major highways. This year I bought everybody Suzanne Somer's *Thighmaster*. On discount. Just as I often find myself talking to the very person who has treated me poorly and I don't recall forgiving them.

English 750 (6 Credits)

There's a saying which goes "the longest trip in the world is from Brooklyn to Manhattan," which has something to do with why you're metaphorically stuck on the D train. Jenny's from the block only when she's well away; it is hard to take it all down and profess stories are about knowing the faces on a slow Riverside bus, or knowing the kinds of taverns that have rooms with cots in the back, or insisting the stories are, in essence, true—true like the dirt on the hands of the father figure in that pretty girl's story. How to construct her even more in pedagogical terms: who has her books upstairs, who has her as talent/talentless, talking of imaginary spaces all the time never using the word utopic but ectoscopic or ensemble? Salles touristes, angiosperms, pop, poplars like snow and the globe thistles radiate the word (but not the color) blue; hollyhock and queen-of-the-prairies, the neutrality of the hopeful story about the white cat—the cat does not embarrass with thoughts of post-national nations, neutrons or noogies. The cat is not trying to convince the story is true, when it may be in several lectures. Haw-hawing the character or author is just another of many of the same simple co-ordinates: the cat lives and works in Orange County. The producer of the show of the story that ends in the motel or hiccups about how the bees are in the hyssop, the squirrels are in the lavender and the worm-wood's in the still, quotes Emerson and Emerson's meanings are page stuck to page. They will say instead of taking the letter "e" from the dsk st, Jr., stick to blood root and Labrador tea—your father's cleomes or spider flowers. A light white hellebore gargle with a gargoyle and a Christmas rose relaxant under Xmas lights—as land went hooray Greeny when a gallant and a customizer rose readily unto Hollywood lights. Oh you!

Grading policy: it's a long, bumpy T-bar ride up Mount I-Told-You-So, so hang on tight.

Life With Neal

Whoever the idiot was who said, "You can't judge a book by its cover," obviously never worked at a bookstore. I worked at one of these corporate mega-bookstores at Diversey Street on Chicago's North Side for two years and I swear all anyone wants to know about is such and such a book with a "grey cover" or such and such a book with the "drawing of the knife."

What else is there to go on?

It was a difficult two years there because, like most people who end up working in bookstores, I had failed dreams that were haunting me and I wasn't exactly handling the haunting like a champion. Instead, I found a stable way to feed my sense of doom—at a bar up on North Broadway called Friar Tuck's.

God, my last days at that store were like some absurd college play about a Chicago nobody knew. It was the summer of the killer heat wave; so hot in my apartment I looked forward to getting into the fold of the air-conditioned superstore. I can still see all those summer books with their neon covers and the blurb "outrageous!" boldly printed on almost every single one. I was alone much of the time and, getting to the skinny, that was the summer I spent two lunch hours at Friar Tuck's with a reporter from the *National Enquirer*, feeding him dirty information about a certain lovable sitcom star.

Although I took every bit of the $2,000 for the information, it wasn't about the money. Mine is more of a classic American tale. You've probably heard it all before.

Now, everybody in the country knows Albert Colchester, the over-ly-affectionate Neal in the primetime breakthrough sitcom *Life with Neal*. But I may know him better than most—because, after all, we were best friends in high school, went to the same acting school, and moved and roomed together for a brief time in our young actors' requisite days in L.A.

What I want to say is he *followed* me to the same acting school and he *followed* me to L.A. where he—the lucky bastard—was picked up by a prestigious agency after doing a series of ads for a major brewery. That agency was the kind of place where secretaries offer you your choice of bottled water—where you could probably have a cast member of *All My Children* killed, if that's what you wanted. So, that was *my buddy*, Albert Colchester, as the mistaken killer on *Frasier*, as the sickeningly sweet "cereal-guy" in *Friends,* and finally as America's favorite puppy dog, *Neal*.

Of course, every struggling actor in L.A. has their own little dramas of psychotic jealousy. And most of their stories make my tale quaintly Midwestern. You learn to never talk about it. You learn to focus your hate on your best friends. Once, I met Patrick Swayze's brother Ken at a bar in Santa Monica and when I asked him if he ever felt jealous about his brother's success, he made some joke about "I'm more worried about the kind of guy who recognizes Ken Swayze," and copped some easy-out acceptance of his brother's fame and fortune. How did Ken Swayze get so cool with it?

I couldn't get anything. I was turned down for parts that a blind goat or a blind Ken Swayze could play. And when Colby (that's what his pals called him) started to go stratospheric it was like I froze with envy. I wasn't getting call-backs for auditions for ads for hemorrhoids or anti-depressants; I wasn't able to hit my marks in an audition to be a back-ground player in a San Bernardino production of *Richard III*—hoping I might find refuge in the illusion that I was a *thea-tah* person. Depressed I could not be convincing as a hemorrhoidal, depressive court attendant I complained all the time. My agent, whose LaBrea office smelled like an old makeup kit, told me I'd better learn to appreciate the auditions she sent me to. An advertisement for a security systems company and a walk-on for a Warner Bros. show called *Hurray for Heroes* both turned up dry. "It doesn't look like you're in a position to be too picky," she would say as I told her again and again about the projects I wanted.

Let me put it this way: by the time *Life with Neal* became "Must See TV" I had flown back to Chicago.

The Enquirer reporter didn't appear out of the blue. I put in the call to the tabloid about a month after the hardcover edition of Colby's book, *Between Nealtime*, hit the stands. I was deeply shaken when I saw those books pyramided all over the display windows of my near mininum-wage refuge from Southern California. His star power was my secret kryptonite, draining me of the strength to perform the most simple tasks. I certainly never told my co-workers of my connection to Colby and brooked the showbiz aspect of my jealous despair in silence. (AC was, after all, a big home-town hero to boot. The local newscasts frequently celebrated his success as another sign of Chicago's misapprehended pre-eminence.) I looked and looked at the cover of that stupid book: his face cupped in his hands and his sleepy smile, inviting all misunderstood married women to buy, buy, buy. In kiss-my-ass flashes, I'd think I could handle it all but when this woman came into the store saying "Do you have that book? The one with the funny guy?" and I *knew* what she meant —I became more of a *problem worker*. My lunches at Friar Tuck's became more of a lifestyle choice.

My parents lived in a Chicago suburb whose only claim to fame was its scale replica of the Leaning Tower of Pisa. A nice place to grow up and a pretty nice place to leave too. When I came back to the old neighborhood, it wasn't like I'd be checking up on old friends or bathing in the nostalgia of the place I first asked a girl "You wanna skip school with me?" My own apartment in the city was so close to the I-90 I worried about carbon monoxide poisoning. So, I liked being in the more secure, quiet and vaguely moldy space my parents would set up for me in the basement when I came for a weekend visit. Another perfect place to watch cable television and smoke cigarettes, I was happy to be there. I mean, I had to spend some time out there—they were always helping me out with the bills because, as I've been saying, I worked in a bookstore for a living.

Maybe they knew and made the possibility easy to see but I was seriously thinking, with the extra *Enquirer* bucks coming my way, I might live at my parents' house for awhile, maybe take some communications courses at the local college. I wasn't really serious with anybody and the phrase *going back to school* sounded reassuring.

Of course, if I stayed with my folks that would pretty much guarantee I'd continue to not be serious about anybody. That would pretty much be the equivalent of committing myself as a mental patient. That I could live with, but there was this thing with my parents who were always just a little *too* thrilled to point out "Albert's" grand success. It seemed like every time I was on the phone with Mother or Father they were always saying something like, "Did you see Albert on *ET*?" or "Did you see that Albert's going to be the new Batman?" or whatever, and then my Dad would be going on about "Albert Alligator" from *Pogo* and my will to live would be about as strong as Sylvia Plath's at Jim Jones's compound.

And every now and then I would charge back: "I'm sick of hearing about Albert, you know. I know all about Albert; I *lived* with Albert in the same apartment on Van Nuys Boulevard!"

"Now, now," my mother would say. "I know that, dear."

The *Enquirer* reporter was a young guy who was quite comfortable with the charm of Friar Tuck's. He grabbed from a basket of bar popcorn by the handful, ordered Old Style beer, and mumbled about how much better it was to do these things in person. "Nice place," he said, but he wasn't there to charm me: he knew I was being paid and it was my job to deliver the goods. As I dished, he wrote little things in a blue notebook. Two days later we met at the same place to go over the same details in his little blue notebook.

"I feel bad," I said then, thinking I was being taped. "Like I'm just this little *weasel*."

"What has Mr. Colchester ever done for *your* career?" he asked dispassionately. And then, mocking me with *Enquirer* cynicism, "Look at you. Do you think he'll send you an autographed copy of *Nealtime*? Look at you. Maybe he'll let you mow his lawn." He finished up and exhaled loudly, mostly to express just how sad he was to leave Friar Tuck's. Before exiting, he turned and said, "Didn't you also say something about Patrick Swayze's brother?"

"Maybe later," I said.

Perhaps all this would be forgivable if Albert Colchester was some unconscionable show business asshole who stabbed me in the back on his way up to *The Barbara Walters Special*. In my darker moments, I could almost convince myself that once he actually *did* ask me to mow his lawn at his new place in Brentwood. But, it wasn't true: what is really true, regardless of what you've read in the tabloids, is that Albert Colchester is one hell of a nice guy.

But what does that matter?

The issue, to me, was as direct as a dog-bite: why him and not me? Was it all just luck? Or am I really that bad? Except for that *really nice guy* part, he couldn't have been that much *better* than I was. I realize, the way this story is coming off, one would imagine me as some inconsolable warty troll, but that would be unfair. Maybe I'm not as classically leading man as Albert Colchester but I'm not Sir-Oinks-A-Lot. I'm near 6 feet, have dark, curly hair; one agency went so far as to call it a "vanilla Andy Garcia" look—and if by a vanilla Andy Garcia one means "the guy who played Newman on *Seinfeld*" that makes perfect sense. When we were nobodies hanging out at the bars in Santa Monica, I always did better talking to women than AC did.

I could live with how I didn't make it as an actor. Failure has a bland mathematical inevitability, like arthritis or baldness, so what are you gonna do? What I couldn't live with, as I started getting those birthday cards that joke about getting older, was how everything I never did was held up in contrast to you-know-who. And the man's not just somebody who won a Kiwanis Club election or published a book of kinky poems, he was a *TV STAR*—and you can't hide from a TV star anymore than you can hide from Richard Hatch's hairy nuts.

The article came out in August. It was a front page panel, not quite as impressive as the main panel about Meg Ryan's "World's Most

Expensive Plastic Surgery," but in lurid yellow letters the banner hurled: *TV'S NEAL'S FLING WITH MARRIED WOMAN. NOW HER HUSBAND THREATENS REVENGE!* The inside article, with a picture I gave them, started "TV funnyman Albert Colchester plays it sweet and innocent on his hit TV show but his recent love life has been no laughing matter . . . In an exclusive to *The National Enquirer*, a close friend of Colchester claims . . ."

I brought the paper into work so I could leave it lying around the main counter. One of the full-time wiseasses took a look at the cover and moaned, "You don't actually *read* that crap do you?" Bookstore types live for moments when they can say things like this.

But I defended the veracity of the paper. I said to the wiseass, "Sure some of the articles probably don't turn out to be true but they all have *verifiable sources*." I had been thinking of my intellectual defense of my snitchery.

"So you mean if some lunatic claims that Oprah Winfrey sleeps with a box of vealchops that's considered *proof*, or *honest journalism*?"

"Something like that," I said to the wiseass and went for a break.

The real fireworks began after I learned Colby was coming to Chicago on his book tour. And just our corporate luck, he was coming to the bookstore's North Side franchise. Celebrity-signings by media stars are the biggest literary events in America and our store was promoting this one to the hilt. "If I don't see a line-up all the way around the corner, it will be a failure," the store manager nervously predicted.

I was closer and closer to asking my folks what they thought of the idea of me coming back to live with them. On my day off, in the midst of an important phone conversation with my mother, just when I was about to ask, she started gushing about Colby's homecoming and how she had told some of her friends that she knew him and if I could help and *blah blah blah*. I seized up inside; not quite mad but I still hung up, happy to breathe the car fumes of my little apartment for eternity.

Later in the day, I made like I was ill and I went home to sleep (I slept a lot those days). Lying there in the late afternoon I started thinking about a play I was part of back in Junior College. The play was called *Lakeshore Drive* and I was playing the role of a big city Mayor's heartless son. Anyway, I had trouble with the big, weepy scene and the director—"famous" for having directed 4 episodes of *ALF*—got all fed up and told me: "David, you don't seem to realize that it's not *just* about saying the lines and walking away looking good." What a bastard he was for saying that in front of the whole cast and God, how I wanted to shove my inevitable success in his face. I slept until the stink and noise of my apartment once again became so unbearable I had to get out.

I showed up to work the next day smelling like Friar Tuck's and the floor manager came up to me, brandishing a small piece of yellow paper and said, "You *know* Albert Colchester?"

"The TV star?"

"No, the ballerina, nit. Of course the TV star."

"Yuh, uh, we went to acting school together."

"*Acting* school? No kidding! I didn't know you went to acting school—although, it might explain a couple of things. Anyway, we got this call from his "people," as they say, and they left this number asking if you—specifically you—could call him before tomorrow's signing."

"Probably needs some help spelling his name," I said softly before taking the paper. In a louder voice I asked if I could take an early lunch which ordinarily would have been a you're-already-this-close-to-being-fired no-can-do but now *I knew somebody famous* and that changes everything. I was better than me: I was Colby Colchester's friend.

For lunch I went to Friar Tuck's and I was the only person there—except for Randall who worked the afternoon bar. I like to think about him as the kind of all-right guy who didn't much care about you unless you had something to say about the Cubs, but he really was the kind of guy who was always saying bug-my-ass things like "You look like shit," or "What are you doing here?" Still, we chatted about some stupid things as other regulars wafted in as the temperatures soared outside. Before I knew it, I had been there for 90 minutes and I said to Randall "Can I use your phone? I'm going to phone Albert Colchester."

"Prince Albert in a can?"

"No. Albert *Colchester*, the TV star."

"Well, don't be too long," he said. "I'm expecting a call from David Carradine."

I left that one, took the phone from under the bar and dialed the number on the yellow paper. Colby answered the phone himself, right away, which really threw me because I was expecting to have to run through a gauntlet of his "people."

"Uh, hi, Colb it's..."

"Hey Dave, how's it goin'?"

"Not bad. Where are you?"

"I'm at the Omni Hotel"

"Oh, the Omni," I said, like I had a private suite on the 90th floor.

"Oh yeah, we're all going to be on *Oprah* tomorrow morning, before the signing."

"You're going to be on *Oprah*?"

"Oh yeah, the whole cast and everything."

"Is it true that she sleeps with a box of vealchops?"

"What?"

"Ahh, nothing," I said, my voice stumbling into the first awkward silence in the conversation. It was all happening too fast. Like an audition, I was off my marks again, bumbling lines I should have had cold. He was still a nice guy. We both said something like "So what's new?" at the same time and laughed and fell back into yet another awkward moment.

"Look, Dave," he said, dropping all pretense. "I just want to know, did you really sell that ridiculous story to *The National Enquirer?*"

"What story?"

"You know. The one about that married woman, who by the way, *you* introduced me to when *you* dragged me to the Bigfoot Lodge. You remember, the one whose husband is looking to shake some money out of me?"

"Is that the story?" I said, "It probably was the husband. You don't actually read that crap do you?"

"Right. Look, Dave, I know it was you and I'm not going to sit around here worrying about all the little secrets you have from those days—I know the truth—it's not like I sit around here blaming you; I just feel bad about the way things worked out you know, like, for you and between us and everything."

"Hey, Neal, do you want me to mow your lawn or something?"

"Look, man, I said I was sorry."

"Not really." I said in my most dispirited, gravely whine.

"Oh God, forget it. I'll see you at the bookstore, okay?

He persisted, "Okay?"

"Okay." I said and hung up.

I looked around the bar in a panic. I had honestly forgotten where I was.

I didn't go to that book signing but I'm sure it was wildly successful. Same goes for *Oprah*. You can tsk-tsk my predictable cop-out but I still look back at that summer in a positive way. Let me put it like this: I didn't move back in with my parents, I didn't pretend I was going to go back to school, I took my two thousand bucks, got the jump on a million geriatrics and I moved to Florida.

I don't talk about it anymore—I left there looking good and now it is over. When somebody says "Do you think this is *Life with Neal*'s last year?" I just shout like a loon "I sure hope not! I sure hope not!" and leave it there.

I have a great tan, I work as a clerk in a video-retailer's warehouse and I write a regular newspaper column about Tampa-area theater in a Tampa-area newspaper. And just last year, I met a woman who is only slightly embarrassed by my life story. She's in the video-business herself. You can tell by looking at us that we are very happy.

What else is there to go on?

Trial (by Matlock?)

From the opening statement:

"Whether or not you feel Doreen's life was worth living depends on how much you like spaghetti. Of course, we know much more about carbohydrate addiction these days. We may feel pity for those who have not learned, the way we pity those who do not carefully recycle, those who waste their votes on third parties, and those who went to see *Godfather III* and claimed they loved it. However, it is not illegal. Doreen just loved the stuff: maybe at first it was because pasta was cheap, and as a struggling oceanography student, it was all she could afford. Later on, when she started making money, she just went for a better class of noodle. *Conchiglie, ditalini, mostaccioli*—it was a beautiful time."

The issue of *Doreen West v. City of Atlanta* did not seem like propitious case law when Doreen West walked into my office and said she wanted to sue the city of Atlanta. It was a cold day and I was thinking about a promising sandwich I had in the office fridge, so I said the first thing anyone in my position would say: "But why would we, a small Buffalo law firm, sue the city of Atlanta?"

It was a corker and at each step, my colleagues would say, "is this for real, Milbury? How long before some judge throws this out?" Anyway, according to Buffalo native, Ms. West, the City of Atlanta interfered with her 6th amendment right (her right to privacy) when the city used a picture of her chowing down at an Italian restaurant to promote itself as a culinary metropolis "beyond grits and fatback." Her grievance was simply remedied but she refused any settlement and claimed extravagant trauma. In other words, she would sue them for a claim of 60 million dollars.

On our first trip to Atlanta, Doreen brought a take-away order of ravioli for the plane which I thought crazy, but when I was digging into my *beef stew à la USAir* she was looking like a genius. She took the window seat while I took the aisle. Although she was somewhat impossible to know, Doreen was, in her own way, a woman of exquisite sensibilities. She knew how to snowboard and every other year she sold jewelry at Ozfest. She could distinguish the prose styles of the three Brontë sisters in less than sixty words and I told her when she could bring that total down to twenty words, I'd be interested. After hearing that our in-flight movie featured Sandra Bullock as a dance instructor I asked her if she knew how to read the bumps on my head.

She worked her fingers in my hair and made foreboding noises. I thought I heard her say something about "arteriosclerosis"—a word I was sure she'd be quite familiar with. The flight attendants looked at us the way Dr. Zaius looked at Taylor—with suspicious disbelief. To make normal, I asked her more typical passenger type questions, but she was impervious to small talk—even if I tried to make the small talk pasta-related.

Despite Georgia's history as a haven for people from English debtor's prisons, its recent legal history has its own mojo: reaching for extra-constitutional authority to protect "peculiar institutions" one century and leaning on heavy prosecutorial authority in order to get quick, hard death row convictions the century after.

We met with some students who were going to work with us and one of them said, "I heard the State hired famous defence attorney Benjamin Matlock to act as a special defender."

At night we would play croquinole with the law students and it was not very good croquinole. The students drank too much and, in the mornings, presented bizarre briefs for strategy. One presented a note to me, in the middle of cross-examination, which read Mr. Matlock's suits cost $2,000 apiece—that he pays a company to wear them in, so it looks like he has only one suit! I could see that as good summary information to feed the jury, making Matlock look even dumber, but it was odd when the chief advertiser for the offending restaurant was on the stand. Another note, more enigmatically, noted "Avoid using the verb *to be*."

At trial I never heard Mr. Matlock's opening remarks and I never looked at the jury. I feared the lunacy of the case and how much I cared. I daydreamed of beds of gnocchi in oblivion.

Mr. Matlock grilled the photographer as if he drove the Manson family up the Hollywood Hills and made issue of the testimony we took from him.

"Did Mr. Milbury promise you anything?" Mr. Matlock asked.

"Well, it's like he thinks he was God's gift to the law, like he *invented* all the big words. And he kept me up late, man, and he borrowed money to play cards."

"Your honor! Objection," I yelled; "It's not like I'm in insurance!"

"Overruled! Where are you going with this?"

Matlock said he could care less if we all died virgins; his hero, Immanuel Kant, he said, never did it once. So if you see a tape called *Immanuel Kant's Doggy Style*, it's likely to be apocryphal. It had nothing to do with what I was saying. I was concerned when the judge instructed the jury: "Ladies and gentlemen I want you to disregard the facts the accuser has presented and pay careful attention to everything Mr. Matlock is insinuating." From the stand I could see through a window outside. Matlock came after Doreen with an ardor that would embarrass Pepe LePew. He had been eating raw linguine—we both could tell.

From the City's cross-examination of the plaintiff:

"Ms. West, I've xeroxed your diary and passed it around to the jury. On page 30 you note parenthetically 'I'm lookin' good,' on page 53 you refer to Veronica Lake as 'Lana Turner,' on page 71 you impugn Mr. Milbury's legal advice, on page 80 you misspell 'parallel' and on page 121, in between thick marinara sauce stains, you write, 'I don't know if I can go on living like this.' I ask the jury if these are the thoughts of a woman that is suffering from trauma or looking for a free ride from this great state?"

Dear Mr. Milbury,

I want to thank you for all your help in the lawsuit—a cause that was noble and true. I have since applied for a job at a canning company in Pennsylvania that has a good record for hiring women. I used to look down at canned spaghetti but now I see its benefits. There is no pre-tension in a can of *Mac-N-Meat-Mania*.

I get to sit in the mountains on the weekends. In the mountains there are many beautiful secrets. I miss the water and my oceanographic studies. The sea wrecks are so pristine: the hulls can be filmed but those who went down are absent, not even their bones can be viewed. Not many bear teeth at all. So much is left unsaid. So much before dummy Matlock, before the spaghetti, before I knew the difference between plaice, cod and tuna. I know I've done something terrible. Something that makes the stunted pines and blue mists on the hills heavy with tuberculosis.

Love,

Doreen West

Street Noodles

I loved Elsa Folson best before we were a couple. When she'd push me off across a car seat or outside her door; when she would hear me opening up and would say, "If you want to keep it a secret, don't tell me! Don't tell anyone!"

You tell somebody something in confidence and do so gladly and with faith. It is safe. But, time goes on, and who knows? A Saint Patrick's Day party here, a silent treatment there, a new friend and a new recreational drug to share and suddenly that old confidence is held by somebody else—and, soon enough, everyone who wants to know. Only a fool would believe it is otherwise.

Like my friend Colin during the summer between high school and college. That's when he told me how his brother, who no one had seen in years, actually had a sex-change operation. Colin was nearly in tears when he told me this—the confusing pain it had caused him and his family written all over his face and trembling hands. It took him *hours* to tell that story and I had to swear a dozen times upon my life, upon my Grandmother's life, that I would never tell a living soul. But, after Colin called me a "scam-artist" when I tried to sell him my old stereo, I never saw much of him anymore. I left for college and incrementally, I confess, I told some people about "the ol' snip-snip" even though I swore I never would. Luckily, by the time I ran into Colin again, three years later, all forgiven on the hi-fi front, the fate of his older brother had become a "hilarious" staple of his regular routine. I swear, within minutes of meeting someone in a bar he'd be going "Oh yeah, my brother had his wiener cut right off! Now he goes by the name Kiki."

I wasn't as lucky with Elsa.

But, after a woman tearfully admits she's leaving you to "find herself" and after you find out how that meant finding herself beneath a bartender named Palmer, why would you continue to be the keeper of her secrets? I only wished Elsa had authentically deep secrets. Like maybe she had a half-brother who was in an Alabama prison or she once wrote a series of stalky fan letters to El DeBarge—but except for making fun of the name *Palmer* I had nothing on her.

Or, at least, that's what I thought when she was screaming at me in front of everybody on Fullerton: "How could you! How could you tell my mother! You fucking stupid loser!"

At 28, I knew I was not a huge success but I didn't think of myself as a *loser*. Still, I confess, on Saturday nights, in Chicago, just outside a stretch of bars at the University, I kept a little hot dog stand.

While my old high school friends were buying Dodge Caravans for their ever-expanding families or having their first books published, I kept a hot dog stand. A stainless steel 16-gauge, 3 bay, hot dog cart that I would have slept in if I could.

I'm sure I was the only American-born person in the street food trade in all of Cook County and, to make it all the more odd, instead of selling franks I sold lo-mein noodles. Gingery, spicy Chinese noodles, fried-up and stuffed in styrofoam containers for 2 bucks a shot. In Chicago, where people need to have tomato and pickle and celery salt on their dogs, noodles were easier on condiment expenses. The noodles were popular too—what with all the University vegetarians who still needed a shot of greasy starch after a night at the bars.

Along with another part-time job I had answering phones, I felt I was doing pretty well—a capitalist in the truest sense. In weaker moments I thought of my own empire of noodlewagons: of bringing my brand, *Street Noodles,* to curbsides from Miami Beach to Puget Sound. However, my dream ran headlong into my unambitious side and by the time I even checked into trademarking the name *Street Noodles*, largely at Elsa's insistence, I found out a restaurant in Venice Beach, California had got there first. Maybe it was a relief: I took more shifts at the telemarketing trough and began to say, "Have you received your free gift in the mail?" with a bit more zippity-zing.

When Elsa finally left, she took a lot of things I ended up missing—

even if, at the time of her departure, I was shouting "Take it! Take it all!" Most of all, I missed a chintzy dinner plate that my mother and father bought for us when they were in Matamoros. The plate was blue and white, rectangular, and had three dimensional ceramic frogs anchored at each corner. So when Elsa showed up on Fullerton, screaming like she was in a traffic accident, I thought right away—*The plate! I've got to get that plate!*

"Do you still have the plate? The one with the ceramic frogs?" I asked in the middle of her indignations.

"What?" she said, losing her place.

"The dinner plate with the ceramic frogs?—Do you still have it?"

"Ya, I think so," she mumbled, before refinding her place. "Do you even know what I'm talking about?"

"I'm just trying to find out if I can get that ceramic plate, Else. Can I come by and pick that up?"

"No, you can't come pick that up!"

"Why not?"

"Because you're a fucking jackass—and if I see you I'll smash that thing over your fucking head."

She looked good screaming like that. Watching her walk away, it seemed a miracle we were together even for a second.

As I calmed down and threw a new batch of onions on my grill, I realized the best thing I could do would be to just wish her well. To let her go and, if I ever ran into her again, years from now, I'd simply apologize for all I once did to make her so angry.

So, I tracked her address down through an internet detective and within the week I went to her apartment determined to get that damn ceramic plate.

She lived in a high rise on a busy street near Lincoln Park. It was the kind of place we would have once made fun of. The kind of apartment where people come in and out with business sections and poodles folded in the nooks of their arms. It was hard to believe that this was the bartender's place. There was a doorman and I asked him if Ms. Folson was home this afternoon because I had a "special delivery" for her.

The doorman said wearily "Who knew gyro stands delivered?"

Working with noodles all day, I had to accept I would occasionally give oniony-oily offense and laughed at the sarcastic jibe. "Ms. Folson," he intoned on the intercom, "did you order something from a gyro stand?"

"Tell her it's Street Noodles."

"It's a Mr. Noodles, Ms. Folson."

"Yes, tell Ms. Folson Mr. Noodles is calling."

"Send him up, Tom," she said.

"Thanks, Tommy!" I said, patting his back and bounding towards the elevator lobby as if I was just allowed to breeze past the line at Studio 54. It was embarrassing when I had to go back and ask Tom to remind me what Elsa's apartment number was, but old Tom was cool about it.

"Well, well, if it isn't Mr. Noodles," Elsa said when I came through her door. "Come in, but don't sit on the sofa or anything! You smell like a hoagie."

"Else," I said; "I don't want to fight, I've just got to get that ceramic plate—you know, for Ma."

"*For my Mommy,*" she said mockingly. "I don't know where the stupid dish is."

"But you have it, right?"

"Well, maybe it's around somewhere," she said, making a wide sweeping gesture as if to indicate the *Showcase Showroom* of her current luxury. Her apartment was beige, warm and tastefully eclectic: a modern couch set, antique wood coffee tables and print posters of French movies. The idea that Elsa was sitting there watching French movies with the bartender, or whoever she was sharing this place with—and this was clearly a couples' apartment—kind of made me feel ill.

"How did you get my address, Stevie? That would almost require a sense of ambition."

"Jesus Christ, Else—do you have much more material left?"

"Oh, forget it. You have no idea why I'm mad at you, do you?"

"I assumed it was because you're upset with how much time your current boyfriend spends on the internet looking at pictures of Justin Timberlake."

"*Ne ne ne ne ne ne ne ne,*" she mocked again. "Don't tell me anything, okay?" she said, but then, as if possessed by a new series of zingers, she went, "Look: if you can guess why I am mad at you, I'll give you your Mom's plate back. If you can't guess, I'm going to throw it right from the balcony here and into the street."

"Come on! I have no idea why you're mad—you're always mad and I always assumed it was because you're completely crazy. You could be mad there's so many flavors of Coke now. I mean, *Vanilla Coke*—come on!"

"No. I'm mad about something you told my mother. My mother!"

"Was it about how you smoked pot with your English professor in the hot tub he claimed he bought for his wife?"

"No. It wasn't that—and I told you, nothing happened there."

"Was it about how you refer to your sisters as *Whore One* and *Whore Two*?"

"No. And, sadly, I think my mother may have actually started that one."

"Was it about how you were going out with that bartender, Poofer—because that was a true story."

"Perfect," she said, "you're out of guesses." She went into the kitchen, came out with the frog plate, opened the window and calmly threw it out, frisbee-style, saying "It's yours."

I imagined the dish braining some old lady getting out of her town car and I screamed: "You killed somebody! You killed somebody! You killed somebody!"

"This is the second floor—and it's in the pool, Noodle-o. Now don't say another word. Just, please, get out of here before I have Tommy call the cops."

It's hard to say when I realized I never knew much about Elsa. We had terrific fights and she didn't seem to care if I had a weenie cart. But if I have to pinpoint a time, I would say it was when I was in my sad undies, diving into a Parkside swimming pool to retrieve a plate that likely retailed for seven dollars.

Resting clearly in the middle of the pool, the plate was still in good condition. The only thing which broke off, in a few pieces, was one of the ceramic frogs. The broken off frog parts were a little more to the deep end which took more of a determined retrieval effort. By then,

Tommy was standing by, helping me pinpoint the proper diving spots. I was proud to have retrieved each little piece even if I was told by a man wearing a red tunic "That was the most pathetic thing I have ever seen. I hope the chlorine killed the gyro smell."

I was uncomfortably damp on the train to my mother's place in Waukegan, but I was hopeful that after presenting her with the wedding plate, she'd help me fill out the gaps in my wardrobe at K-Mart's socks and underwear department. So, later, I sat right in my mother's kitchen, trying to glue that broken frog back on, while Mom looked on with disbelief. "That girl was always a little hard to understand" my mother said, lighting up a menthol cigarette.

As I glued pieces on, trying to reconstruct the frog, I asked my mother if she ever talked to Else's mother when we were a couple. "Maybe," she said, "something at one of those memorable times when we would go to Pescara's together and Dad would entertain the Folsons with his Señor Wences impersonation. *S'alright.*"

"Amy Folson? Amy Folson?" my mother said. "I think she might have phoned after Elsie took up with the bartender. Something about how she had hoped you two would get married and give her grandkids. I told that foul-mouthed bitch right there and then how you said Elsa never wanted kids—and the reason why she took up with you was pretty much the same reason why she took after the bartender. As a way of avoiding all that. Let's face it, neither one of you were going to tell her she had to settle down."

"I have a rule," she said, "if you want to avoid commitment, take up with a bartender." My mother was always taking things from life and extemporizing them into one of her "rules." If she mistakenly received Manhattan clam chowder instead of her preferred New England she would say, "I have a rule: it's not chowder unless it's New England." Who was I to contradict the rules?

Much like driving and preparing for a proper job interview, gluing things together proved to be one of those regular chores too taxing for my independent spirit. Taking a break, mother waited for me to make her a Vodka-Collins Mix while she muttered, "A hot dog stand. Stevie, Stevie, Stevie."

The repaired frog on the dish looked ridiculous—more glue than ceramic. At best it resembled a funked-out sheep; at worst, a piece of gum. Still, it was good enough to find its place back on Mother's hutch and to inspire a long monologue from her about my parents' day trip to Matamoros. "You know your father never talked much," she said, "but it was a great day. I have a rule: when in Mexico you have to buy over-the-counter prescriptions. Next time I go, I'm going to buy some over-the-counter Paxil and some over-the-counter Paxil inhibitor."

I'm not sure I ever believed the conversation between our mothers was the thing that inspired Elsa to rip into me that summer afternoon on Fullerton. It was too much like the *single gunman* theory, and sometimes wondered if it was something else, some wild superfluous nipple accusation Elsa falsely attributes to me. Maybe I should have apologized to her, as I should have apologized to Colin for blabbing about his brother-sister. But, when winter came and I timorously put a FOR SALE ad out for my "Asian-seasoned, 3-bay lunch wagon" I felt like I had apologized enough.

I took a full-time position as a telemarketing supervisor which meant taking young minimum wagers aside and telling them "I have a rule: keep them on the line." And when a particularly determined young phone hawk would want a good lead I would always include the name and number of a certain E. Folson in Lincoln Park and I would tell the kid: "You get her to talk!"

Keglomania!

I did not make it through college. I convinced myself and bragged to my friends that I was a "creative person," naturally oppressed by the constraints of deadlines and required readings. So I left university in the middle of my first year.

That was back in the eighties. All my professors then were swinging, erotomaniacal intellects who constantly made appeals to our glands to try to get us interested. My English profs were particularly keen on presenting all literary artists as sexpots. How depressing it was to learn that William Shakespeare—perhaps the biggest geek in the history of the world—was getting more than me.

Epilogue

My 35th birthday fell on a Friday in June which was a bad day for any of my lame friends to get together, so, to make up for it they would take me out for lunch on the Saturday. My closest friend, Ed, told me that he had met somebody I "should meet" and he would try to "bring her along." I hated being fixed up and hated the idea more since I had lost my job three months previously. Picturing my future as some dude washing cars, I dreaded being asked what I did.

When Ed and the woman sat down, Ed went: "Why don't you tell Sheila here what you do."

Embarrassed, I went into a monologue I canned awhile back: "You know, Ed, *sloth* is under-rated. Does Santa even care if you work hard? No, he adjudicates strictly on a *naughty/nice* ratio."

"I mean, Protestants are always going on about how Jesus was a carpenter and that means we all should work hard. But, how do we know that Jesus was any *good* as a carpenter? I mean how do we know if the word in Galilee was, sure, if you wanted your water turned to wine Christ was your man, but if you wanted a new wall-unit you were better off seeing Abdullah the carpenter down the street? And *why* on earth did Christ have to work? I mean, did Joseph take him aside one day and say, "you know my boy you should learn a trade in case this *Son of God* thing doesn't work out?"

"That reminds me, did you see the story about how this art gallery accidentally broke some precious ancient tablet which had Jesus's family tree inscribed on it? That was terrible, terrible news: I never knew Jesus had a brother! Apparently, the tablet revealed, Jesus had a brother named "James." Jim. *Good Ol' Jim Christ.* Talk about sibling rivalry. I mean I was jealous when my brother had a 3-speed bike, but— even though that was a sweet ride—he was no Jesus. I bet you Jesus's Dad Joseph liked Jim, probably hung out in the workshop with him all day saying things like *you know Jim, I don't know about your half-brother, if you ask me, he has a lot of artsy-fartsy ideas, your mother spoils him, thinks he's too good to help out in the shop—but, Jim, you're all right with me!* Good Ol' Jim—I bet you when Joseph hung out a shingle *Joseph Christ and Son, Cabinetmakers* he was talking about Jim, what with Jesus being busy touching the feet of lepers."

Ed, to his credit, stopped me there just before I got to the bit about how Jesus's having a brother was probably worse on Mary and Joseph's relationship—because that would mean after Mary had God's baby, she had Joseph's and, like, how's Joseph going to compare to that? I mean, God probably knows about foreplay and everything. Or, being God, the ladies don't complain so much if he seems in a hurry. Anyways, I can imagine this might have tortured Joseph and he would get all snivelly and pouty during sex: *How's that Mary? How's that? Am I as good as your fancy man?*

Ed's intercession didn't matter, though. The woman was repulsed by my demeanor long before I gave her a chance to be unimpressed with my appearance and my spectacular joblessness.

What was I doing since losing my job? I wasn't writing, wasn't rediscovering my creativity. I had, however, become familiar with daytime television. I knew Barney the Dinosaur's soothing voice and knew what books Diane Sawyer thought highly of; I knew that if you're thirsty in Port Charles you shouldn't go to The Bucket of Blood. I could joke about how tacky *Live With Regis and Kelly* was, especially in light of Kelly Ripa's attempt to be on every single TV show, including my fave soap, but *Live . . .* was my favorite. The *real* truth of what had happened to my life, what I did, only became clear to me on the day of my 35th birthday: it was sad and embarrassing and I am not proud to admit it, but I had a crush on Kelly Ripa.

It was a hot afternoon and we ate at some outdoor, Californian café in the Marketplace. The woman excused herself to some made up event and a few of my other, old friends had shown up, but my birthday had largely been forgotten. They didn't want to say anything that might bring up the story of my ugly dismissal from my lousy job so they kind of avoided me. They all nervously drank Amstel Light beer; it was an Amstel Light kind of crowd.

I met this other woman named "Julia." She looked nothing like *La Ripa*. Ed said "Julia is a big tech at H.M." and, though I had no idea what H.M. was, I understood it had something to do with computers. (Ed worked reading manuscripts in, as he put it, "the fuck you department" of a publishing house.) Conversation at the table just would not take off. When I finally said something, still thinking of my previous monologue, this is what came out:

"You know what my favorite part of the *Bible* is? The one where God gives birth to Santa—and Santa rises from the manger to say *Behold! For I am your God!* and then Santa, like, gives presents to the wise men and the donkeys. That section of the Bible always soothes me."

"Ha!" Julia went. "You ever see those people with those bumper stickers that say *My Boss is a Jewish Carpenter?*"

"I have," I said. "I never understood them. I mean, I always thought they were very nice—but that it was just some guy who was proud of his boss. But what about the rest of us who didn't have such great bosses? Where are the bumperstickers that say *My Boss is a Vengeful Alcoholic* or *My Boss Thinks She's My Mommy?*"

Most of my lame friends cleared out after that exchange yet Julia, to my surprise, stuck around. My conversation skills did not improve after they left me with this woman who seemed oddly determined to not be disgusted by me. "I've always wanted to beat the crap out of one of my friends," I said. "I mean, these days, the only people who you can be certain are not carrying a gun are your friends ..."

I was braced for an awkward silence but she just put her drink glass carefully on top of a napkin and said, "Your friends are full of shit."

That Julia sure knew how to sweet-talk.

We took an afternoon walk and started to get along. We walked a good stretch of the city, past the State House and well onto the waterfront, where Julia lived. Feeling romantic, I pointed out to her all the places I had been mugged. When we were at her place she told me her life story.

She said she was a refugee from a polygamous community in Arizona. When she was 17 her father made an arrangement for her to become the third wife of a 56-year-old man who was pretty big in the polygamous world. It was Julia's suggestion to marry this man: she liked him and thought it was, relatively speaking, a good career move. Still, sometime before the wedding she began to have doubts. She didn't like his other wives, she was frightened about children, she had never really seen the world. So she shipped out of the desert mountain community and moved to Seattle where she worked at a Tully's Coffee, went to the University of Washington, and went on to help co-ordinate the computers in the Arts departments of Boston-area universities. She said she still considered herself Mormon but not a Latter-Day-Saint, whatever that meant.

Why people told these stories to people not named Oprah was well beyond me. Was she going to kill me for my biblical indiscretions? I was glad she wasn't there for the whole *Jim Christ* debacle. Whatever, I had to admit, her story sure made my life-defining story of meeting Carl Yaztzemski at the Medford Plaza Mall seem less impressive than I thought it was.

She took me to her room—and we did it without music or wine. By the time the sun had slipped away from her bedroom windows, we were wide awake and it was still early enough. She took my hand for a second and said, "Why don't we take my car out and go for a night drive? *Let's go to the beach!*"

O sweet Mormonetta, what was there to say but *yes*?

It was an hour drive so we stopped at a convenience store outside of town for supplies. At the counter I saw a display of *Redbook* with Kelly Ripa's face on the cover. I asked Julia if she ever watched *Live* ... and she just said, "I hate those fucking idiots." In my mind I could see Kelly winking at me from that magazine, as if to say "*What a wicked day!—take it to the hoop, superstar.*"

The Northshore Beach was not one of the more popular ones. Basically, it was just a wharf with a corn-dog stand and a group of out-staters in pink teri cloth. We gawped at the panoramic vista of beach as the sun set, but we did not walk the surf in the post-coital bliss I assumed would be ours. "Did you want to go in?" I asked, meaning the ocean.

"Oh, for heaven's sake, no!" she said, with an air of assurance that changed everything. At that moment, the sun sinking off past the cran-berry bogs to the west, let me know this whole thing was going on in her head and had nothing to do with me.

By dark we went into some beachfront bar with a corny, Irish-themed name (Paddy O'Barley?) and inside, she went a little kookier. "You put some songs on the jukebox—I'm going to the bar," she said. While I admittedly took too long to make the choice to basically play Abba and Backstreet Boys songs, I was surprised when, once I was done, I saw that Julia was doing shots at the bar with some tall dude wearing a puka-shell necklace. "Red Hots," he said, as I interrupted them, "*Absolut Peppar* and cinnamon schnapps." Dude was pretty slick, he ignored me the way a big brother would, got Julia to play some pool and, before I knew it, he was dancing with her to one of the songs punched-up on my quarters.

Abba's "Dancing Queen" had come full circle: from camp ditty to retro pinnacle and all the way back to pure embarrassing crap.

The place was crowded with locals. I wasn't thinking about being dumped or feeling jealous of Puka Shell Dude. But, his hand just above her Mormon ass, a thumb in the belt loop of her jeans, I just thought, "There's my ride—my ride!—how the fuck am I going to get back to the city?"

After the slow-dance Julia came up to me and said, "We're going to go shooting." The Dude lifted up his shirt and revealed the wood-fin-ished grip of a .45.

"Shoot what?" I said, trying to be cool, but thinking I would soon find myself being chased through a cranberry bog and soon after in the same support group as Ned Beatty's *Deliverance* character.

"I dunno," The Dude said. "Truck tires, stuff, telephone wires. Stuff."

Julia laughed and said, "Anyways, I'm not going back to the city tonight—but I'm sure there'll be someone here who is. I think there's a bus even."

I didn't want to get mad because I was afraid The Dude would shoot me and say "Wicked pissah" as I expired in front of his eyes. In fact, when I said, "it's only a $100 cab ride." Dude went, "Hey, I bet you're one of those fuckfaces who memorizes routines from *Seinfeld*." Julia smirked at him admiringly.

"You can't just leave me here," I whispered to Julia, hoping Dude would not interfere.

"Sure I can!" she said. "Some lose their faith completely—I'm just ditching some guy I met this afternoon."

That is exactly what she did. I sat at the bar for awhile and wondered if I would ever get the nerve to ask someone—"Say, are you in from the city? Mind if I hitch a ride back? It's been months since my last stabbing." I hung tight to the bar, still terrified about the gun. A bogus Irish band (McWrath and the Taters?), were ready to take the stage.

The night air was damp, smelling of sand and onion rings. There was no excuse for why I didn't just steal her car and take it back to the city myself. But I didn't—I had enough juice left on my Mastercard to get myself a room at this beach place called Spinnakers Motel and I left a message for Ed to come pick me up in the morning. It was a nice, if chigger-ridden, room. The TV worked. It was the kind of place where nobodies are shot all the time and I grimly thought my life had finally come to where only the solemnity of prayer could help. I put my head against the bed and wondered what to say.

Dear Lord, in your wisdom you saw to it I would never become the creative person I once so desperately wanted to be. In your wisdom you saw to it I would be over thirty-five and jobless, stuck in some shabby, beach motel with a layer of dead flies in the window sill; you saw me here to where I would be terrified of the locals and utterly alone; but, thank you Lord, O thank you for allowing me, on my birthday, to have had sex with an authentic crazy girl! I had sex with a really crazy girl! Thank you O Santa! Thank you for Kelly Ripa too!

I closed the blinds to the "ocean view" (you could see a patch of it past a boarded-up bumper car pavilion) and went to bed. The next day was Sunday and *Live...* wasn't on.

Road Porn

When I was a kid, my father would take me and my brothers out for a drive in the country—allegedly, just for a hot dog or a swim. But, before we departed on such adventures, Dad would share with me a crucial part of his traveling philosophy that I've kept with me to this day. He would take me aside and say: "You're not getting into my car again unless you've taken some *Gravol*."

So, I was a sleepy kid, unimpressed by the roadside oddities and local attractions my father was so jazzed on. Like the place that mixed coke and root beer and called it *root-a-cola*. For Dad, nothing could slake the thirst aroused by a long summer of hard work and being nagged at more than a tall glass of *root-a-cola*. Even a local production of *Young Abe Lincoln* or a historical plaque that commemorated "the first ski school in Tamarack county" seemed to impress him. But when you're a kid, all that's a bore and all you care about is finding a place to swim. It didn't matter if you were at the Four Seasons or at the Interstate Discount Motor Lodge as long as it had a pool. Having to listen to some pimply-faced guide intone *here we are at the site where Benjamin Franklin invented the first onion ring blossom* was torture— you're a kid, who cares? My brothers and I were always asking, "Dad, are we going to a pool? A pond? A sprinkler system?"

Though sometimes I think my father would have saved himself much aggravation if, instead of hauling us away from town for a day to see the grave of a racehorse, he just hired some neighborhood punk to keep a hose trained on us throughout the summer. We would have been happy with that and who knows what Dad would have got up to? Maybe he would have made it across the Mississippi, maybe have had an affair with his company's sexy receptionist, the one that scandalized the company's annual Lake Fest Picnic by wearing what my mother called a "French cut" bikini. "How could anybody wear something like that—to an office event?" she questioned my father as if he put her up to it.

Nobody should ever have to answer as many questions about baby blue swimwear as my father did that summer, but he hung in there, as he always did, saying the words that often resonated in the background of our childhood: "Marjorie, you're being ridiculous."

My younger brother Sam doesn't reminisce as much as I do and certainly never about the experimental theater that was Mom and Pop, but he was the only one of us who kept to the road, who saw things my father only dreamed of. He has lived in the north of England as well as in Paris and in nearly every corner of America: he's been a bank teller in Atlanta, an East Village poseur, a toll booth attendant off the Straits of Michilimackinac, a short order cook in St. Louis's Hill district and, twice, a sponge—living off some rich girl desperate to prove how much she hated her parents (once in New Jersey and once in Santa Cruz). He always tried to keep in touch, keeping a game spirit and a typically cheerful tone.

So, he was pip-pip jolly when he phoned me at my Boston apartment on an early August night looking for help. He said he suddenly found himself in the "sad valley known as Canoga Park, California" where he was living with a struggling actress named Amanda Mays. He could hardly contain himself trying to explain, hemming and hawing about a fix that struck him as both tragically odd and naggingly hilarious—a fix my little brother had a peculiar knack for. Sam said about a month before, he was working some joe job outside of Dallas, Texas and he "had to leave that area in a hurry." But, before he did, he left a silver 1988 Plymouth Acclaim in a city parking lot which had, in its trunk, he swore, up to $30,000 worth of brand new DVD porn. "Top quality porn, Steve," he said to me. "Big stars, big names, the very best companies."

I could tell what he was asking but I let him sweat it out. How many times must a brother say to a brother: "If you want me to take a parking ticket and go out to Dallas and then drive a car all the way out to California so you can retrieve your suspicious boxes of porn you have to ask!" He kept alluding to the *high quality* of the DVDs, mumbling some-things about "masters" and how it would all be *totally worth it*—but I would have done it for free even if the trunk was full of laundry. While I joked I wasn't sure, saying I hadn't been out west since "that time I came back with a recipe for high-fiber margaritas and a provocative tattoo of Mexican wrestler El Santos" the truth was I was incredibly honored Sam asked me to execute this absurd plan and that it involved something as glamorous as 30K of porn made it all the more exciting.

I agreed to take the parking ticket.

Thrilled, we just started clowning on the phone, riffing on the filthy things I usually held back on in my polite Boston circles and which were the crucial bond in our fraternity. Sam and I may have never become the musician or writer we were supposed to become but we knew the difference between a *Dutch oven* and a *Cleveland steamer* and we weren't shy with each other about bringing everything back to that crass level. In this spirit, Sam seized on my suggestion I might keep a travel diary to get the old creative juices flowing and said: "The only wisdom I can impart, Stevie, is that travel diaries are immediately spruced up when you replace the word *rest* with *Russian whore. I stopped by the hotel for a quick Russian whore. It had been a long day and a Russian whore would be just the thing I needed. It's surprising how refreshing a 10-minute Russian whore can be.*"

The parking ticket came by courier along with a copy of a new transla-tion of Dostoevsky's *Notes from Underground*—Sam's favorite novel. However, having the financial security of your basic Wendy's floor man-ager, flying immediately to Dallas was out of the question. So, I did the only sensible thing: I phoned our older brother Doug in Connecticut and asked him (and one of his fancy-assed cars) to join our conspiracy.

"No fucking way!" was his first response, followed by "Are you two ballscratchers out of your gourds?" but I had confidence he would come around. Doug was a lawyer in the New Haven area. After working for a long time strictly as a corporate consultant, he switched practices and now, for the first time, was arguing felony cases before juries. It was hard to keep in touch with him even though he was always attached to a phone. I admit Sam and I made fun of him and his dorky Christmas cards, inevitably with a picture of his pretty wife, Virginia—who every-one called *Jinx*—and their three beautiful kids, Janey, Marshall and Elaine. But, we knew he wasn't as straight-laced as we'd make him sound.

In fact, the conventional aspects of Doug's achievements were prob-ably in direct proportion with his sense of anxiety and unease. When we were kids he fantasized about war—Vietnam in particular. Considering he had a black MIA-POW flag over his bed where his first Heather Locklear poster should have been, I always thought Dougie showed great restraint never going on some paranoid militaristic spree. Since college, he poured every bit of himself into his work and if Jinx heard he had such an opportunity to loosen himself from this mania, I'm sure she would say, "Dougie, you go with your little brothers to get that porn!" Jinxie was great that way, keeping Doug connected to fam-ily responsibility. I'm sure it was the threat I'd talk to Jinx about this road trip which finally had Doug agreeing to drive me to Dallas in his big Jeep Cherokee and where he would, he said somewhat grimly, "drive back alone."

Actually, as Doug had an annoying habit of addressing his buddies by vaguely testicular sobriquets like "What do you say Nutsy?" or "Hey there, Dingleberry," he actually said: "If you can get the time off, Nardsy, let's yee haw our way to Texas. I'll even buy you your bus tick-et here."

Yee haw indeed. Who could resist all that porn? And Nardsy had plenty of time.

With depressive certainty, the road seemed the only possible reme-dy left for a life which had been ground, I was convinced, to complete shitdust. I had separated from my wife more than a year ago and only her "busy schedule" kept divorce papers from being finalized; I started smoking again and had gained quite a lot of weight—to the point where people in the street usually referred to me not as *Nardsy* but as *Big Guy. Hey, Big Guy, you got some change? Hey, what's up, Big Guy?* It had been a long time since I put away my guitar and, then, my only source of income was writing about Boston's music scene (such as it was) for a local alternative newspaper—an alternative, that is, to the kinds of newspapers that cost a whopping 75 cents to buy.

The bus to Connecticut smelled like a mix of wet burlap and corn chips. Before I left, I wrote two columns for the free paper and told them I'd send one from the road if I went long. I thought I'd enjoy the melancholic staring out of bus windows that life's dissipated losers are born for, but I found the ride more about seeing the grit in the eyes of working people. All these people who were putting in solid hours at the onion-slicing factory, trying to better themselves by enrolling in Professor Boring's book club, elated to get a beat on how to chase squirrels from their aging mother's lawn. I was a whiney freeloader in their world—not unhappy I wasn't flying onto a New Haven helipad but sad I couldn't quite fit in with the crowd. Not the working guys who ate their sandwiches slowly, not the cute backpackers who listened to their Discman discs contentedly.

Jinx picked me up at the Greyhound station, saying "With the way you talk I expected you'd be the size of Pavarotti."

I said: "Does that mean we can or can't go for subs?"

At some local lunch stand, Jinx told me the jury for the trial Doug was working on was still out, and we'd have to wait in New Haven till they came in with a verdict. So, for 5 days I lived in their townhouse, never seeing much of Doug or his slicked-back hair. I divided most of my time between their hot tub, playing board games with the kids, and staying up very late in the basement watching old movies on cable. My first night, I watched an old Warner Bros. movie where a porky Alan Hale Sr. hands a character simply known as "Irish" a glass of champagne and says, "That ain't beer, Irish, so don't guzzle it." I did not want to guzzle—it would take five days to get the stink of my apartment off and I loved each lazy, defunkifying day.

My nephew and nieces were amazing: bright, talented, and never complaining. When I was their age it was all arguments about Led Zeppelin songs and how many tokes of pot did it take before you were addicted to heroin. Where my brothers and I conspired as to how we might score an iron-on T-shirt which claimed "I have the force" these kids were Junior Environmental Awareness Leaders, spelling bee final-ists and participants in the State Wide Constitution Challenge.

One afternoon, playing Yahtzee with Janey, the oldest, I started ask-ing what bands she liked, thinking Uncle Tubby would impress her that I actually heard of a few things. She liked most things—hip-hop, new country, even the boy bands. She thought the sexy girl groups were "all right" but preferred new sensation Dena Garnette whose hit "You've got to love yourself (because you will never change)" was that summer's chart buster. She thought Dena's message was ultimately more positive because it was based on a power that comes from inside, not how one dresses. Such bright insight made it hard to concentrate on defeating a child at Yahtzee. Janey took the shaker and thought about what she said and after rolling added, "but, they all dress like idiots!"

By the time Doug came back to say, "It's time to hit the road, Nutty" I had figured out what games his kids could beat me at even if I was trying. Winning was something I think they greatly enjoyed. Just before we hopped in the truck, Jinxie took me aside and gave me an envelope with $300. She said, "This is for you—when you see him trying to phone the office, or to 'check his e-mails' use this to prevent that from happening, okay?"

Doug had one of those headset cell phones and he pretty much talked on it all the time as we drove out on our first day. We only went as far as Philadelphia so we could hang out at the Sheraton with two guys Doug went to law school with. And those boys loved to talk shop: they argued case file in the lobby, argued case file on the streets, argued case file when wiping off some of the Velveeta cheese from their pant legs when having a cheesesteak "for old time's sake." Every now and then one of these guys would try to involve me, invariably asking me what I did. They'd listen to me explain how I kind of lived the life of an undergraduate and they would look at me with the pitying consternation of veterinarians. I'm sure they assumed I was gay. It became a late night, the lawyers getting hostile with their fancy scotch knowledge. *Ah, order the Glengoorhan ya case of ball rot.* Maybe with "Scotland the Brave" on their minds, we went to this place on the Southside which featured a jazz musician who played the bagpipes. It is hard to describe the sound of hearing bagpipes—ordinarily used to indicate the deaths of clansmen from several countries away—played indoors and with a jazz combo at that. But, I still harken to that night, when I want to feel sober about the resilience of the artist. For who ever embodied artistic drive better than the jazz bagpipe player?

I realized traveling with my brother was traveling with my brother and it wasn't going to be *On the Road*—or even *Dumb and Dumber*. Kerouac, as far as I knew, didn't start a cellphone conversation every twenty minutes with the phrase "Nutty! It's Doug. . ." I didn't say much. Mopey, I felt like the sick kid in the back of the car "ruining" everyone's trip to the world's tallest wooden roller coaster. I remembered how my Dad would light up when he said before we went swimming we were going to some small town's "Tomato Days" festival where, he promised, you could eat a tomato "like it was an apple." Of course, I ended up only eating a hot dog with ketchup that tasted like ketchup, refusing anything in original tomato form. How I wished I could have been shaken out of that sulk, that I could go back and bite into one of those apple-like red tomatoes, its seeds and juices tickling my chin as they rolled onto my white T-shirt, my father proud of my fearless tasting of life.

Luckily, the jazz-piper brought the evening to a migrainey end. Doug and I cabbed back to the Sheraton where, in the fancy room, I grabbed a can of beer from the mini bar and put the old movie network on. In *The Bigamist* a fidgety Edmond O'Brien is married to both pretty Joan Fontaine and sensible Ida Lupino, with some nice intrigue as to when O'Brien will be caught and a considerable attempt to not make him look like a sexual rogue. In one killer scene, O'Brien meets someone (an official of some sort) who has discovered his secret and, with a sharp, clipped accent, he says to The Bigamist: "I don't know how I feel about you. I despise you. I pity you. I wouldn't even dream of shaking your hand but, somehow, I wish you luck." I'm dying to say those lines to somebody.

Outside of town the next day, having a breakfast buffet at some Amish-themed restaurant called Old Dutch, I kept repeating the lines. To which Doug said, "How can you watch crap like that?" That was Doug. I could start a two-hour-long conversation with Sam by saying, "Hey, in the movie *Freebie and the Bean*, who played *Freebie* and who played *the Bean*?" But if I asked Doug, "Hey, in the movie *Freebie and the Bean*, who played *Freebie* and who played *the Bean*?" he would look at me and say, "Shut up, nutsack."

But at that moment, amused by bus boys who were either Amish or just dressed as Amish, I decided it wouldn't bother me: we were on the road, just about to wing past the Mason-Dixon line and we were eating shoo-fly pie for breakfast, how could there be a problem?

We bombed down I-81, the Shenandoah Mountains bobbing along our left flank, Doug way over the speed limit and talking just as fast into his headset while I stared off to the right, counting miles on the longest stretch of Virginia. By dusk, I had my first shot at the Jeep and, as I promised I would, I took us straight into the heart of some town looking for action, something—anything besides the I.

After stalling through construction traffic, we stopped by a local diner called The Mason Jar, quite proud to advertise its *Free sweet tea with River Fish special.* We sat at the counter and ordered two specials. There were lots of guys hanging out—ball-capped locals who we assumed were trading secrets over coffee on how best to flush frogs and turtles from the river beds for late night snackin'. "Where you fellers from?" the hairiest of these guys asked me and as soon as I said "Massachusetts," I thought I might as well have called Hank Williams Jr. a big fruit. But, despite whatever *Hee Haw* nausea I was filled with, he said, "Jeez, that's great—I was there a few years ago, do y'all get to see many games at Fenway?" and things like that. I certainly did not mention how in my circle, we took a dim view of *Go Sox* Bostonians and disliked the final encroachments Fenwayites made on whatever music scene was left around Kenmore Square. I just asked him if there was anything special going on in this area of the state, a concert or a bar that we could go to before settling down.

He chuckled and said a few of the guys in the county were headed to The Pea Ridge, a bar just at the Tennessee border. "It's a good place," he shrugged, saying it was to be host to an annual homemade bikini contest sponsored by a large international distillery. Alas, he never referred to the place as a "honky-tonk," but he talked about the kinds of drink specials they had, how they played good music—"not just country music"—until very late at night and that the jalapeño poppers were really hot—as if I wasn't completely sold by the phrase homemade bikini contest.

It was still quite a drive from the The Mason Jar to The Pea Ridge but with Dougie back behind the wheel we made it through the early night, down state and right up to the big sign that read "Bikini Contest Tonight." The Pea Ridge was actually a motel bar, right by the curl of a dark off-ramp. We checked in and even took a little down time before the contest got started. It wasn't the Sheraton, it wasn't even up to EconoLodge standards, but it did have two beds and offered a great chance for us to get so bombed we would not notice any other missing amenity. The bar itself was dark: painted purple with New Yorky graffiti as purposeful decor. Neon lit—the kind of lighting used in strip clubs which masks skin imperfections but aggressively highlights dandruff and false teeth. It was already pretty crammed when we got there but rather than being the jocky faux-Hooters we expected, the crowd was eclectic and alternative in the truest sense. The Pea Ridge, it turned out, was a kind of omnibus social club for those who walked outside local propriety—a welcome spot for lesbians, goths, bikers, punks, knuckleheads and pillpops.

A guy at the bar who picked up on my northeast accent said: "Hell, if I could marry my truck in Massachusetts, I'd vote for Ted Kennedy myself."

My river fish sat well, Dougie wasn't calling any of the locals "Old McGonad's Farm" and the beer flowed as the locals took the stage. Introduced by a self-consciously ironic host in a black Elvis wig and a pink tuxedo, the girls took two walks across the stage in the look which I think defines America: swimwear and heels. Oh, we approved wholeheartedly of Odelia's "warning tape delight," generously applauded Dana's "tin foil tankini;" were amazed at Shirl's "crocheted tinny-cans"—Bud for the top, Busch for the bottom; said hooray for Myrtle's faith that being next-to-nude would quell suspicion her itty-bitty Mountain city outfit was store bought; but the whole room exploded with glee when Tammy bounced around that stage in her "possum string special."

Now, who knows if the yellow-white fur on that piece was really possum, but on Tammy there was no doubt who Doug and I would be voting for. When the pink tuxedo'd mc sang, "There she is—with the best homemade bikini in the Tri-City area" we felt justice had been done and, as the supreme court would, we ordered lots of beers. When the music came back on, everybody in The Pea Ridge, including the fabulous runners-up, seemed ready to rock. At some point a tall guy who claimed he was Tammy's boyfriend brought us beers and said "I want to thank you fellas for voting for Tammy," and we took the beers and Doug immediately toasted "To democracy!"

"To democracy!"

At some point, well after I unsuccessfully tried to convince Tin Foil Dana to hang out with us, they played Led Zeppelin's "Rock and Roll," and we got up and danced. I couldn't remember the last time I tried to move in rhythm—maybe strange for someone who used to bother anybody unfortunate enough to share my breathing space with claims I was born to be a musician. I was so shy and hung up about music in high school I certainly would never dance to music I thought crappy. How happier I would have been if I just asked the girls to dance to those dopey Phil Collins songs they wanted to dance to. Did they want anything more than that? The magic of The Pea Ridge wasn't the girls in swimsuits, after all, but the release of some pretension screwed on so tight I suddenly found it hard to talk to nice people. That or the girls in swimsuits.

We did shots as they turned the house lights on and left the backway, straight into the hotel, to pass out on the beds. Elated at what we had done so far from home, I flopped on my bed and said: "Dad would have loved that."

"God, he would have *loved* that," Dougie said as he flopped on his.

Whether or not our father would have actually loved The Pea Ridge I wouldn't know. Dad was always pretty sober. Sometime, when Sam was in Europe and I was just in the city, my mother died from a pulmonary embolism. It was sudden and horrible: her body found in the nature section of The Hampshire County Public Library. We all drew around Pops at the time of the funeral—Sam moved back to the States and never returned to Europe. In the months following her funeral I saw just how much he grieved for her, his whole body, from sunken cheek to wobbly ankles, collapsing with the loss of what he was sure was "the one honest thing in the world." How helpless he was, how desperately in love, as he yelled out "Marjorie!" whenever he was left alone. Not more than 6 months after she died, my father had a series of strokes and died on his way to an Amherst hospital. His last word was "Marjorie!"

I assume every keen American traveler has their own signal for where "the real South" begins. For some it's probably where people immediately ask "How y'all doin?" for others it's probably where NASCAR circuit stars are given the same adulation usually reserved for boy bands but, for me, there's no greater sign you're really in the South than when you see your very first roadside boiled peanut stand. And somewhere in the central part of Tennessee, long after rushing out of the motel to avoid a late check-out fee, long after the gas, coffee and pie — in the hot sun, by an Interstate off-ramp, underneath a big beach umbrella sat a grandmother and two kids with a big steaming kettle and a handpainted sign that read *Boild P-Nuts*.

Boiled peanuts are kind of like little boiled potatoes and they're slippery, hot and difficult to eat. It may even be more difficult to eat boiled peanuts while driving in downtown Nashville traffic, looking for the nightclub where Dolly Parton first performed, but I did not let that stop me from trying. "Give it up, Van Testes, watch out for the fucking traffic" Doug said as I couldn't quite find the clutch, soppy husks all over my arm. Not only did I find the club (hard to miss even if you're trying to shell soppy goobers) the parking gods blessed us with a ready space so I eased the Jeep on the Lower Broadway curb, bounded in, ordered up some beers and listened to some hungry hopefuls playing early sets. Doug lagged behind, talking into his head set—he waved off any beer, having had so much the night before.

I slept off the early evening in the passenger seat as we pulled out of Nashville and didn't wake up until we were pretty close to Memphis. The Jeep had taken on the daunting aroma of unhappy peanut-eaters. To Doug's relief we were too late for any Graceland-related stuff and his office booked us into a nice hotel just off Beale Street. "It's been a good day," he said, "nearly getting killed with you behind the wheel, listening to hillbillies who think they'll be the next Gomer Brooks . . . anyway, while you were passed out I phoned Sam and cleared the air a little bit."

"What do you mean?" I asked, never realizing they had some air-clearing situation.

"Oh, we had a falling out a few years ago. You remember when he was in the East Village working with 'the Collective'?"

"Of course."

"Anyway, I saw him in the city all the time around then, would treat him to lunch at the Oyster Bar and at some point he asks me for a pretty substantial loan and, you know, it looked like he needed it, so I said sure and gave it to him just like that which may have been a mistake because it probably looked like I had so much to spare it was like tossing him a quarter. Still, I gave him the money and never mentioned anything about repaying, but that was all he could talk about and it became as if I wanted to have lunch as a pretext for loan collection. Anyways, he would get really belligerent and political as if I was Simon Legree and he was Mahatmafuckinghandi. So, right there in the Oyster Bar, I let him have it, telling him how ashamed Dad would have been to see him like that and that was it. He stormed out of there and I haven't talked to him since."

"Wow," I said and kept quiet as Doug pulled the Jeep into the hotel and let the valet have the key. I could understand why Doug would never have mentioned this, but I felt ill knowing Sam never mentioned this to me at all. I didn't know how Doug could trust the valet. "Hey," I asked Doug, "did Sam give you that whole rest/Russian whore routine?"

"He sure did. I told him you were having a Russian whore while I was driving."

That night, we walked the Beale Street scene. I can think of nothing worse than going to some expensive "Blues club" on that strip to listen to "Mustang Sally" with Wisconsinites in their *Snoopy State University* T-shirts. But, it was beyond hot at night and we found some backyard terrace where they played rock music and, lordy lord, sold beer in 44 oz. cups.

On our way back to the hotel I picked up a large pizza slice and just as I was about to bite in, we heard what we assumed was a gunshot. We assumed it was a gunshot because everybody screamed and dropped what they had in their hands and just ran. We made it halfway up the hill to the hotel when we realized it was all a false alarm and everybody was heading back to pick up anything they dropped. I half considered going back to get another slice. How I regretted dropping that slice—I was too tired and too full of peanuts to feel excited about putting the mini bar's macadamia nuts on Doug's bill. *O, Slicey, I will remember thee!*

It took some determination but I did convince my big brother it would be pointless to have come all this way and not have breakfast at Graceland. It wasn't as exciting as I hoped but maybe that had something to do with how I was feeling, mumbling each step of the way "No more pancakes, no more beer." Worse was that there were no tour guides because we worked up this whole routine where we'd ask the guides "Did Elvis like Chinese people?" And when they told us Elvis loved all people from everywhere be they Black, White or Catholic, the other one would pretend to be unrelated and ask, "If Elvis invited strangers to Thanksgiving, how many Chinese people do you think he would invite?"

When we were by the King's grave Doug was on his headphone, saying something like "You wouldn't believe all the Scrotum-swingers here." I didn't have a camera but wanted to do something so I left the copy of *Notes from Underground* Sam gave me which I finished after I woke up early for a bit of puking.

"I am a sick man . . . I am a wicked man."

Things were going fast on the road, every other minute some radio station was playing Dena Garnette's "You've got to love yourself, because you will never change" and I was really getting into it—losing all my indie cred with glee. But, I was overindulged and singing for the end of a part of myself. When the Jeep broke down just on the state line road of Texarkana, a fuel line spilling all out onto the street, I nearly wept with a sense of helplessness. Dougie took it all in stride saying into his phone: "Sue, will you patch me through to a AAA service in Texarkana, Arkansas or Texarkana, Texas—it doesn't matter which. When I'm on the line with them you may want to get me the numbers of some local Jeep dealers." Then Doug was talking to some AAA dude who promised he'd be with us "in a jiff."

I'm not sure what made me so restless then, but when Doug innocently asked me whatever happened to Grace (my wife) and "what went on there" I finally let go of the ridiculous illusion of *we just grew apart* and *we discovered we wanted different things*, and I sat there in the flashing Jeep, telling the whole story. Grace taught at a major university and during one winter term she started hanging out at one of her student's apartments—*Angela* was a good student but in some kind of trouble as she was being harassed by this big brute of a guy, also a student, who was coming around to Angela's apartment at all hours calling her a *bitch* and a *slut* and whatnot—scared the bejeezus out her, just because he couldn't handle rejection. Anyways, Grace and Angela developed a kind of *mother-daughter thing*, especially as Grace would wait over there so the cops could come put tabs on Ol' Johnny Date Rape. Around exam-time she confessed that she was, for the last year, actually sleeping with the alleged bully and "Angela" was just a student in her class whose pretty hair she was jealous of.

"Wow!" Doug said, "I would have never pegged her as a skank."

"Neither did I!" And that's what killed me, what really dragged me down: I mean if I was with her because I thought she had the greatest ass in Somerville, I might have thought being sexually undercut by some dude was a terrible but understood consequence for a marriage based on such a sublime rear end. I was with Gracie because I thought her sweet and incapable of hurting me and maybe that was unfairly naive but, once that illusion was broken, I could be her friend, her accountant, her ticket scalper, whatever, but I couldn't be her partner. Besides, she moved in with the student to some place in Brookline.

I went on and on about what happened, like a Valerie Bertinelli character in a Saturday afternoon movie, while the AAA guys hoisted the Jeep and took it to a local garage. I went over the details in the hotel we would stay in and again in the Waffle House we would eat at, until AAA fixed the Jeep's hose in the morning. Dougie was really sympathetic to the plight as he saw it and even offered to get me an escort for the night, "a little *Texarkana puttana*" as he put it "to get you back on track." Tempting as it was I just ate my chicken and waffles, found an old movie (Alan Ladd as a San Francisco killer) and tried not to think of the smell of gas or Gracie's busy fall fucking schedule.

Doug said, "You know, Steve, if that's how it is, you need to get your life together and concentrate on a new relationship, maybe one that is more based on the ass. The ass doesn't lie and, little brother, yours is really starting to tell a whale of a tale."

The Jeep was fixed before I was up. Doug was pretty happy about it all, saying he could have fixed it himself if he only knew what to do. Putting on a corny accent he promised we'd make it to Dallas "quick as a Mr. Jackrabbit humps Mrs. Jackrabbit" and he had us booked into this really nice modern hotel and everything. "Modern hotels" had rosemary mint shampoo as opposed to the more economical root killer brand. It was going to be great, but I felt remorse for having gone on about being the kind of fat loser whose wife cheated on him with a student. I nervously reminded Doug what I told him was on the hush-hush, and I was sorry to burden him or anyone with such old news, but he should keep it to himself. "Nonsense," he said, "privacy is bound to the same illusions as the Maginot Line—this is what I tell my clients: if you tell one person, I don't care who it is, you might as well just yell it from the rooftops."

"In other words you're going to tell Jinx all about this?

"I told her last night, when you were running the shower so I might not hear you upchucking—so, what, are you bulimic now?"

"I wish!" I shouted. "It would take resolve to puke myself thin— I'm just not feeling well."

"Well, let's saddle up—a little root-a-cola and we'll be on our way."

The anticipation was so high, we drove straight from our morning gas n' waffle stop to the Dallas parking lot where Sam's porn-loaded Plymouth Acclaim sat. Dougie paid for the keys and the $210 parking fee. "That's probably worth more than the whole car," he shrugged. He gave me the keys and said "well, you better get used to driving this thing so why don't you take it to our hotel, and we'll check out the trunk in the parking lot there?"

I got lost in Dallas traffic a few times before I found The New Trinity Plaza and my brother was pretty steamed it took me so long but right there in the hotel lot, even before we checked in to our fancy digs, we popped open the trunk and saw the three tightly packed boxes marked Puritano Distributions. Dougie took his keys and cut into the packing tape popping up a flap which revealed, as promised, DVD after DVD of XXX Hollywood porn. It was beautiful. He flipped through a handful of DVDs like they were baseball cards in a prized collection: *Chloe Cums First, Succubus, Naked Hollywood, DJ Groupie, Intercourse with the Vampire, Perfect Pink #9, Never Quite Enough, Wet Weekend, Hi-Infidelity.* "Cool!" he said, "Now I know how the first visitor to *El Dorado* felt."

Then, to my surprise, he started to drag a box out of the trunk and upon realizing they were deceptively heavy he asked for a hand. I helped him take one box and put it into the trunk of the Jeep. "What are you doing?" I asked.

"Oh, I'm taking one of these boxes with me," he said with a self-satisfied grin.

"Did you talk to Sam about this?" I said like a big nerd.

"Sam'll be fine with it," he gleamed, slamming the Jeep's trunk down, "he doesn't owe me anything anymore."

"I just don't want to get into trouble."

"You worry too much, Nutty," he said, "you've got to concentrate on having a good time—so let's check into this fruity hotel, okay?"

He was right, of course, so rather than think about what the fuck I would say to Sam, I shifted worries. I was good like that. Thinking I would lose my job I took out my notepad and got a local paper and started tracking what was going on in the local music scene. On the pretext of my business, I dragged Dougie to a section of the city known as Deep Ellum and we checked out five hyped local bands: Must Muster, Lem Townhouse, The Agoraphobic Wilburys, Summer Stinkler and Horshack's Addiction. Could there be worse names? It was quite the slog through all the bands, boucing from club to club, pretending I had not come to the age where I found it too loud, pretending I identified with angst in songs like the Stinklers' "Suburb-O-Virus." And going through the pretense of interviewing the bands afterwards, listening to their profundities—*corporate rock is, like, bullshit*—when Doug said, "Let's get out of here!" all I could say was *Amen* even though I knew it would mean hitting some leather-tacked, jazz-infested scotch parlor.

Scotchies was just that bad. A piano player tinkled all known boomer strains, from Billy Joel to Fleetwood Mac, while men and women laughed as they tried to sing along. I personally know of no sound more disturbing than drunk people singing "American Pie." Something about the garbled lyrics, the amplified choruses, the use of the word "levee"—it seemed a sure sign you would wake up ashamed. Still, Doug seemed to make friends with everybody there, and at some point he was pushing me to make time with this attractive woman who probably had kids in another state and mostly just to show Doug I wasn't afraid of him or his talky-money world, I chatted her up as if she was an ass model for *Ass Magazine*. When I finally asked her if she would like to check out the mini-bar in my room and dance to my Phil Collins records she looked grossed-out and said, "easy there big fella."

Big fella, big fella. That hurt. Her sharp Chicagoland voice echoed in my head as I slept it off in the modern hotel. Before I fell asleep I thought how lucky Doug was to have all that porn to himself.

In the morning, his hair freshly cut and with a jacket that looked new, my brother said goodbye in the parking lot. Before he got in his Jeep and left me to the Acclaim and the western leg of my trip, he shook my hand firmly, looked me in the eye and said: "I don't know how I feel about you. I despise you. I pity you. I wouldn't even dream of shaking your hand but, somehow, I wish you luck."

In 1864, after the disastrous battle of the Wilderness, General Grant cried and cried in a way that quite distressed his men. But the next day, rather than retreat and regroup, Grant moved his troops forward against Lee's, and that's why he was the Union's greatest general. I was no General Grant and as I pointed the Acclaim out of Dallas, in the dark blue of pre-dawn, I had no confidence I wouldn't just give up. While the American road is the last great refuge for the gross ballcapped fatso, I was beginning to avoid checking my rearview mirror in case I caught a glimpse of what a porker I had become.

I knew all those "pretty on the inside" hoorahs which chicks have learned to squeeze like ketchup all over the hard truth. Platitudes fervently evoked because they are not authentically believed. I knew God had his ways and if he looked at me and said *I'd like to create a cross between Leo Sayer and a large potato*, I'd think it wasn't my fault. But it was: that was the worst thing about taking another trip to the mirror factory in Tubbyton. In the background were the ditched careers, the childless relationships, the *hilarious* nights with hipster friends. What did I have left? Certain discoveries seem redundant, but they come as a shock, like a headline that blares:

Snout-nosed sweaty pigman sad to discover
His rich voice actually more 'oink-like'

Yes, it's quite different down in Pigton—even if there are much worse stories than the ones about me in the easy-to-ignore *Pigton Gazette*.

Despair gripped me as I chugged through the endles scrublands of West Texas, past the spinach fields and oil wells into the mountains knowing it would take a real effort for me to get myself back on track, to have a life I was proud of. The Acclaim kicked its way to El Paso where, after a whole day of sustaining myself on adolescent self-pity, I did what all grown men would do to lose weight and put themselves straight: I drove right into the lot of The Del Grande Steakhouse where, if I ate a whole 72-ounce steak, the meal would be free.

The billboards started sometime around Odessa and since the local attraction of a "beer drinking goat" was well off my path, I let my hunger, exhaustion and shameful determination build. As soon as I told the waitress in her blue and red cowgirl outfit I wanted to "join the Del Grande circle of champions," she clanged a dinner bell and two other waitresses led me to a sort of raised dining area—a dining *stage* if you will. I suddenly knew how Muhammed Ali must of felt when he stood in the ring for his beliefs. Some guy in a grey suit and ten gallon hat asked me my name and where I was from and then pulled out a megaphone and said, "Now lissen up ev'one, we've got Steve here from Boston, Massachusetts who thinks he can get a free meal at the Del Grande Steakhouse and join the Del Grande Circle of Champ-ee-ons. Oh, but Mister Massachusetts, you've gotta show us y'all can handle something more than a bitty bowl of *chowdah*."

It had come to the point where even Texans were making fun of New England accents. If I didn't finish, the meal would cost $64— which didn't worry me considering I let Doug pay for everything up to this point and still had the $300 Jinx gave me to keep Doug off the phone (next time, give me a Luger, Jinxie) in a pristine fold in my right pocket. But I wanted to finish that meal more than anything I ever wanted in my life.

The killer was, along with the four-and-a-half pounds of meat, you had to eat all the fixins too: big french fries and a lettuce and cabbage salad soaked in a pumpkin-orange French dressing. I came out of the gates strong and determined, like Secretariat at Pimlico, victory was a forgone conclusion: the only question was how many records would be broken. But somewhere into the second pound of the meat I started to feel it, and the taste of the meat and fat started to overwhelm me, and when I gave my first push back from the table, veterans at the Del Grande gave a little *ooh*. "Hang in there Boston!" one yelled. After that first gasp I had a small go at it again but I was never the same. There was still a good pound of meat left when I crossed the line which separates *stuffed* from *ill*, my neck muscles sore, my chest tight, a sense my eyes were being crushed by excess meat being stored in my skull. I may have taken five full minutes to chew my last mouthful and when I did this without puking, I signaled I was through.

"*Awwwwwwww!*" the audience went before returning to their normal sized cuts. The man in the ten-gallon hat took out his megaphone and said, "Too bad, Steve. Next time. You gave it a Texas try, maybe you'll tell all yer friends in Massachusetts just what it takes to have your name enshrined in the Del Grande circle of champions." While he was talking a waitress dashed off my bill and put it on my table. The echo of the megaphone piercing my head, staggered by the meat sweats, I put $80 down and headed outside into the steakhouse's courtyard. They had all these fiberglass steer statues everywhere and I stumbled through the plastic herd until I came to a field's edge, where some blackberry bushes were, and I slipped and lay there, hoping to bring up some of the steak.

I must have fallen asleep somewhere in the back of that bovine statuary. All I know is some woman in a white cardigan sweater with long curly hair shook me to, saying, "Mister, mister, are you okay?" When I stood up, brushing the blackberry bush detritus off me, I said I was fine. She sort of laughed and said, "Why don't you cool off inside—would you like to have a coke with me?" So back inside the place of my great shame, at their little bar called "The Bull Pen," I shared a coke with the petite woman who rescued me. Her name was Pauline and she was very nice, obviously familiar with the excess of the steakhouse and even asked, "Why would you even try to do something like that?" I finished my coke and thanked her and to my surprise she asked me if I'd like to meet her in town, she was going to hang out with these two girlfriends of hers and take a walk around the plaza of the old city.

Her two friends were just as nice. I think she said something about them being nurses, and the four of us just quietly walked the plaza, talking about the things people talked about, I guess: what did one make of the latest *Survivor,* how best to *Support the Troops,* how old-timers referred to the square as *Alligator Plaza.* When I started talking of my travels, of course editing out any reference to how I may be the unwitting middle man in a transaction of hot DVDs in the *Dirty Debutante* series, I said I hoped to make it as far as Phoenix the next day, Los Angeles the next, they all seemed to get excited because a friend of theirs, Katie, lived in Tempe, and I would *love* Katie, they said—I *just had* to meet her. I asked them if they wanted to go for drinks but they all said they had to leave and they wished me the best. Pauline wrote Katie's name and number down and folded the paper into my hand, intently saying, "You give that girl a call, okay? You will never meet a more beautiful woman." And as I walked toward the 1988 Acclaim, my savior shouted again "Call her!"

"Okay!" I said, "Okay!"

Walk the streets trod by Billy the Kid a brochure gamely campaigned, *Visit the world's smallest bookstore* a billboard suggested, *Amor Escandoloso* a *2-por-1 Tecate* strip club beckoned, but I stuck to the beauty of the Interstate. Rushing through New Mexico and into Arizona meant I'd get into Tempe in good time and still find the nerve to phone up my Katie. It was weird, sure, and who knew if they weren't all pulling a scam which would eventually see me walled in an Arizona basement—but why should I be so cynical? People got fixed up all the time, didn't they? I mean, that's what people did. They phoned each other and they went to Jennifer Lopez movies and shared desserts and said, "We should do this again," even if the whole experience fell well short of the fantasy fueled by a Meg Ryan or a Ron Jeremy.

I became so anxious with anticipation I phoned her from a gas station in Tuscon. As soon as I explained just who the hell I was she went, "Pauline told me about you! Hey there—are you doin' okay today?" And she had just that kind of twangy voice, like she was used to telling people good news. So I asked if we could get together for dinner or a movie and she said, "I don't think we'll be going for a steak will we?" and I laughed and she asked me if I knew where in Tempe The Acres was. Of course I had no idea but said I was excellent at finding my way around, which wasn't exactly true but she gave me the address and the simplest directions. I looked around the gas station and saw a rack of red truck caps, so I told her she'd know it was me by my "lucky red cap." "Great!" she said. "You can't miss The Acres—see you at 6:45, Steve."

From the red hats in the store I had a choice between one which read *Truckers Do It On The Road* and one which said *This Rig's Rockin.* Naturally, I went with *This Rig's Rockin.*

Taking a tip from Doug, when finding accommodation I bit on my natural desire for cheap roadside grunge and went for the rosemary-mint shampoo. Splurged for the big double bed too because, apparently, a feller from Boston can give it a good Texas try. I sat in the hotel tub for a long time, hoping the fancy soaps would more than wash me—they would *marinate* me in their exquisite richness. Truth was, I had never really been on a date before. Before Gracie came along, my only girlfriends came to me in more classic city mixers where alcohol and despair preluded our unforeseen relationships. I was giddy, laughing to myself. The chivalry of American dating was completely foreign to me but, if syndicated television programs like *Blind Date* or *Fifth Wheel* were at all correct, I knew you inevitably ended up in a hot tub where the girl would gigglingly confess all her past girl-girl dalliances.

The Acres was a large, commercial hacienda—very austere in its Olive Garden squatness—dwarfing a dusty and undeveloped section of a Tempe suburb, itself a suburb of Phoenix. There was a simple sign which said The Acres lit up with desert blue lights right over the portico that led to, I assumed, the restaurant's court yard. A girl with long chestnut hair wearing a white satin pantsuit with faint blue stripes stood right by the portico, and before I could fully say to myself *My God, she looks like a Minnesotan's wet dream* she saw my red cap and shouted out "Steven!" and I took my trucker's hat off and walked closer to her, her face warm as a California peach basket, said, "hello," and she shook my hand and said, "Welcome to The Acres."

"Is it time to go in yet?" I asked.

"Why not?" Katie said, and we walked through the portico to the courtyard where there were quite a few people drinking what looked like beer in plastic cups. Many wore white outfits and they milled about a teeny-tiny swimming pool with big brass rails. You could smell the chlorine. Somebody came and brought us cups of iced tea. I talked intently to Katie, with a determination to appear confident and honest, as opposed to just funny—even if it meant revealing things best suppressed. She listened well and seemed to take no pain in my chatter, even if every now and then she waved to people in the courtyard. This must be a real local scene, I figured and she must be a popular girl—and why not?—*look at her!* "Let's go in," Katie said, as she took me by the arm and led me through a small passageway into a large sun-lit room. Evidently, The Acres was not a restaurant featuring Sonoran fusion cuisine but an evangelical temple featuring a silver poster which promised *One Mightier Than I Cometh.*

I'm not sure why I just didn't run from that place screaming. I was so far off about what I imagined this was all about I think I just didn't want to reveal how stupid I was. *Oh, this is a religious service? I knew that! What, you're here to baptize adults? I knew that!* And I sat there in the temple room as some silver-haired preacher in a white robe led us in prayer and song before inviting everyone back to the courtyard.

The teeny-tiny swimming pool was actually a baptismal font. Its chlorine a saving grace from those whose spirits may have been cleansed but whose underwear retained human imperfection. It was a wonder they didn't have one of those cutesy signs that read:

We don't save souls in your toilet
So please don't "P" in the baptismal

The people in the white outfits, including Katie, were busy lining up people into seated rows. As I was a wretch found asleep in an El Paso blackberry bush after trying to commit *carnecide,* it stood to reason I would accept such a pretty opportunity to be born again. The white-wearers were church underlings who gained favor in the church's presbytery with the number of people they presented for baptism. I looked at the other guys: hobos, ex-cons, druggies—in short, my demographic. And I sat down calmly, just like Katie asked me to. I think I might have gone through it all just to avoid embarrassing her—as if there was still a chance for *us.*

Two church elders began calling out those who were ready to take a dip with the Lord. "Who is ready?" they intoned. "Who is ready to say goodbye to strife and to start a better day?" One by one, a lost soul would look to a white-pantsuit wearing cutie and say, "I am ready!"

Katie assured me all I had to do is say, "I am not ready!" if I did not want to *accept the lesson*.

When volunteerism faded a little, the elders began calling on the underlings to present those they "invited" to The Acres. Katie said she invited "Steve from Boston" who seemed, she said, lost in "a whirl of human despair only the Lord could understand." The elder asked me to come up and take my baptizing like a man.

"I am not ready," I confidently said.

"Not ready?" the elder growled. "Not ready! When will you be ready? When your life of excess has you stretched out in the morgue? When your soul is consigned to hell? Not ready! When will you be ready? When there is nobody beside your deathbed because all those who love life know you died a long time ago?"

"I am not ready," I said, in a weakened, unhappy way and I pushed myself to the portico. Katie came after me, as the elder trained his attention on some other homeless wretch.

"Don't you want to be saved, Steve? Don't you need to come through this day with a greater sense of purpose?" I feebly stammered who among us could know what their purpose was? Didn't Saint Jerome have to whack his chest with a rock every now and then? I'm not sure she knew the reference to Saint Jerome and it was possible behind her white suit, her soft chestnut hair and bright prairie smile was a sobered drunk or reformed prostitute. A swell of vulgarity was building up inside of me—*Go fuck yourself Captain Jesus, Go fuck yourself Captain Jesus, Go fuck yourself Captain Jesus*—but I kept calm.

I said: "Katie, I may go to hell or whatever its closest New England outlet may be, but I'm here in the Phoenix area for the night and I'm just looking for a good taco and a decent night's sleep." Katie said she understood and she hoped the experience, the pressure of the elder, would not sour me on the only *real* love I might ever find. I said *no* but left her and *The Acres,* quoting Dena Garnette:

You've got to love yourself
because you will never change

Around two years before her unexpected death, my mother took a strange interest in turtles. Initially, I think she saw some show on the

Discovery Channel which exposed the turtle's innate beauty in a way which really touched her and soon she was buying coffee table books about turtles and then turtle stickers for her letters, turtle-shaped soaps, turtle contact paper, and an expensive lamp which sprung from beneath a turtle's shell. It was fine by me: in a family full of men, having a theme to gather gift-giving days around was itself a real saver. There were lots of ladies who had things about animals in that way: *sheep ladies, duck ladies, owl ladies, squirrel ladies, elephant ladies, iguana ladies.* Still, until the day she died in the library, perhaps trying to discover more about the turtle, she wore a mother-of-pearl turtle brooch my father bought her as a Christmas present. She was buried wearing that brooch and I think the eulogy had a reference to the hardships of a sea turtle's mother.

It only dawned on me during the trip out west, as I held a little turquoise and silver turtle in my hand at a Mexican flea market in the town of Blythe, California, how odd it was she chose to idolize the turtle. Busy, impatient, and prone to living off unwise passionate conversation, she was nothing like the hard-shelled, longevous turtle. I could have understood better if she loved the hummingbird—the hummingbird was no less beautiful or profound. Maybe she saw in the turtle some quality she knew she lacked, maybe the turtle was steady and impervious much like my father seemed to me. Maybe the turtle knew what it took to keep her happy. For whatever her insistences, her demands that things be a certain way, she never seemed unsure and never lost her ability to laugh. At least she never seemed interested in getting pet turtles and was content with the terrapin bric-a-brac which grew steadily in the last years of her life.

I bought the turquoise turtle and other knick-knacks in the market—sunflower seeds, dried chiles, chicken-flavored lollipops (!!!)—before heading out to Los Angeles and the final day of my trip. I was not used to driving—to say nothing of avoiding near religious conversions—and I looked forward to just settling down for a few days, reading papers and sleeping all day. Having such a late start, taking long rest-stops, the sun was already going down when I was coming through the desert into the Los Angeles area and it was dark when I decided I'd spend an extra hour in the Valley missing my exit on the Ventura Freeway.

I parked the Acclaim in the stone driveway of a small but nice split home in Canoga Park and rang the doorbell, ready to smack Sam a few times out of sheer excitement. I couldn't believe I had made it so far—it was like the successful conclusion to a Matt Helm movie. A young woman with a large, circular face, scraggly hair and what I can only call "Hollywood breasts" answered the door sleepily saying Sam wasn't there. I explained a few times how I was his brother and he was expecting me with the Plymouth Acclaim.

"The one with the boxes?" she asked.

"That's right! The one with the boxes!"

"You're Sammy's brother?"

"That's right! I'm Sammy's brother!" I said, so delighted this woman who I assumed was starlet Amanda Mays, was catching on. She let me in and brought me to the living room and said, "Sammy probably won't be home until very late or very early, but you can sleep on the couch, Stan."

"Actually, it's just Steve—short for Steven."

"Okay, Steven, you can sleep on the couch—there's a tape of the Mary Tyler Moore marathon in the VCR if you want, and I hope you don't mind but I'm tired and I'm going to go in the other room." She wearily shuffled to the back room, a strap of her vermillion thong showing above her grungy grey USC sweats, shutting the door behind her where she started immediately to sob loudly.

I had no idea what to do. Like any dumb guy, I just wanted it to stop and would have told her right then I was *desperately in love* with her if she would only just stop. Instead I crept up to her door and knocked and asked, "Are you okay?"

"I'm fine, Stanley, don't bother—I'll see you in the morning, honey." I'm not sure if she stopped crying or if she just turned her face into her pillows, but I took her at her word and let her be and went at their fridge and then went at the MTM festival tape. I watched maybe three hours of Mary before turning to regular movie TV which I would fall asleep to. There was some old color movie featuring a very young Kirk Douglas who was either out to destroy or save the redwood forest, I can't remember which.

Sam woke me up in the morning, a *venti* Starbucks coffee in his hand. He had a lot more gray hair than I remembered and his face had a weather-beaten leatheriness—his years in the sun catching up with him. He said, "Rayanne said you got in late last night—I wasn't expecting you for a couple of days." He drank up his coffee, even tilting his held back and tapping the bottom of the cup to jog out its last essential drops. "Ah!," he said, "give me the keys, Steve-o—let's check out that porn."

I delayed getting up, thinking of how I'd tell him Doug took one of the boxes. *Let me wash my hands. Can I get coffee? So, Amanda's real name is Rayanne?* That kind of thing, just trying to think of a way to tell him Doug took one of the boxes. What would be the best way? We walked out to the driveway and before Sam opened the trunk I shouted, "Doug took one of the boxes! Doug took one of the boxes!"

He laughed and opened up the trunk and he sort of sang to himself *he took one of the boxes, he took one of the boxes, he took one of the boxes* while taking the two heavy remaining ones out and putting them into Rayanne's hot pink Ford. "Oh well, joke's on him," he said, when it was safely stored in the pinkmobile, "when Doug strokes his way past the top he'll realize it's mostly gay porn."

Later that day, the three of us drove up to where the railroad tracks are and Sam pulled the pink Ford up to a converted car garage with painted black windows and a simple neon sign which flared PUR-DIST. I helped Sam lug the boxes to the front door when he asked me to sit and wait with Rayanne.

We waited for a long time. Rayanne was dressed up now—a tight black mini-skirt—showing out for anybody who wanted to recognize "Amanda Mays" on Topanga Canyon Boulevard. She smoked cigarettes and french-inhaled dramatically. I think the only things she said the whole time were: "What the fuck is taking so long?" and "You know, Steve, you should try wearing lighter clothes—like Gap khakis."

Sam came bounding out like a delirious bunny, singing like Carmine Ragusa "You'll Never Go from Rags to Riches." He drove us out to this seaside Hawaiian bar in Malibu, where he calmly peeled away $2,000 dollars and gave it to me. "For your troubles," he said. The rest of the wad he put in an envelope and gave to Rayanne, saying "This, Ms. Mays, is for you."

She folded the envelope and said, "Come to Catherine Zeta-Jones, my darling."

We drove to Santa Monica for an authentic Oaxan dinner, and walked around the pier afterwards to watch the sun set. The sun dipped sharply, filling the sky with a bright violet haze which bled quickly into the quiet blue of near night. It was a great trip—once in a lifetime, hands to the wheel and I actually made money, no questions asked. But, instead of feeling the satisfaction of completion and the excitement of the Los Angeles nights ahead, I felt a sickly despair. Behind the veneer of little schemes and the beckoning promises of taffy stands on the outskirts of town, were the grim posts of conscious choice—the certainty that, whatever my "hilarious" protest, I actually chose to do the wrong things. I knew if I had the choice to become the happy knockabout musician I said I wanted to be or to become the fattest man in the world, I would always choose to become the fattest man in the world. I responded to the calming beauty of the Pacific sunset by chain-smoking.

I stayed at Sam's place for almost a week. He went out with his friends every night. Sometime around six, Rayanne would ask him "Are you going out with your friends tonight?" and when Sam would admit he was, she would get mad. I assumed she stayed in, watched *Mary* and cried. Sam's friends were a lot younger than he was and they were Hollywood screenplay scam-artists. They talked endlessly about the industry and the legions of assholes who were preventing them from realizing their dreams. Their actual pitches—*Disco School, The Brothers Katsopolis, Staten Island Gun Club*—were so ridiculous they became a kind of stand-up routine, funnier with each taste of failure.

Each night we went to the same place: an English style pub near the Van Nuys airport called The Duke. I never expected anything but callow conversation and ridiculous scheming hanging out with Sam. But it was less cheery than I imagined and I was surprised to see how thick-skinned Sam actually was—it was no wonder he could bounce around from place to place. No wonder he could leave moon-faced Amanda Mays alone each and every night. I had no idea what he did besides drag boxes inside that building and I knew not to ask. One night we all went to see a Black Sabbath cover band on the Strip and somewhere between their sleepy rendition of "Iron Man" and their half-hour version of "Paranoid," I knew I had to go back home.

Two days later I took a late flight out so I'd get to Boston in the morning. Sam was going to The Duke so he asked me if I wouldn't mind if Rayanne drove me to LAX. "That's cool with me, Nutty," I said. He thanked me profusely for driving the car—for the whole trip—how amazing it was to have a brother he could trust. Rayanne drove the pink car and got all dressed up—it certainly didn't hurt to be seen with her. Having bought a pair of Gap khakis at a realistic size, I thought I owed her something. She pulled me up to the curb of my terminal, and told me how glad she was to have had the chance to hang out a bit, that it was too bad Sammy spent so much time at The Duke. I knew Sam wouldn't be in Los Angeles for that long. I kissed her on the cheek and gave her the turquoise turtle I bought in the desert. "It's so cute!" she said.

"Break a leg, Amanda Mays," I said, grabbing my bags out of the trunk.

"You too! Thanks, Stan, thanks," she said, pulling away from the curb. When it was too late and she had spun past the drop-off circle, I shouted out, "That ain't beer, Irish, so don't guzzle it."

I wish I could say that when I returned to Boston, where the country's mornings start, I redoubled myself and became so comfortable with the way God made me, I never once drank too many beers, never once Googled the name "Amanda Mays," or even once stayed up till dawn in a depressive funk, watching George Raft in *Loanshark*. But I can't say that, nor can I say I became so content with my job reviewing music I began seeing myself as a successful reviewer, a nice guy, or whatever booby prize title is held onto by those who know it all zoomed by too quickly. What I can say is I lost some weight (basketball), kept all my deadlines, and started hanging out more. I dated nice women who were sometimes fun and sometimes desperate but, in the main, just as perceptive to the indignities of reality TV as I was. I even picked up the guitar just to prove to my friend Julie how I knew the chord changes in Cheap Trick's "Surrender." I half-heartedly tried to become a kind of travel journalist but my ideas, like "Where To Get Stabbed and Stabbed Fast in Phoenix," were brushed off quickly by an editor who said, "Why would our readers want to read this?" That had me thinking: "Why wouldn't a *Boston Globe* reader want to visit an abandoned sugar factory and a chicken restaurant that boasts *no habla inglés*? Has New England gone mad?" But, still, I traveled more, if mostly to the Amherst area where we were all born and raised. I thought of going back there and I thought about proposing to Julie and renting a van for all our stuff. Standing over my father's grave, I thought he would be glad to know all his boys had been west of the Mississippi and I had, at least, seen Robert Mitchum's star on the Hollywood Walk of Fame without throwing up once. Whether he'd be disappointed, as my mother was, that I provided no more grandchildren, I couldn't really guess. No children. Who knew if that would ever change? Most of all, I think what I learned, after my great road porn trip, was always there in the lyrics of Dena Garnette: *You've got to love yourself because you will never change*. A tough lesson for an American man who just turned 40.

By the Same Author:

Self-Help Books
-*Daily Affirmations for the Dead-Beat Dad*
-*I'm all right, You're all right and Other Half-Truths*
-*If Sitting Around the House Wearing Nothing but A Cowboy Hat and Pashmina Scarf is Wrong, I Don't Want to be Right*
-*What Would Urkel Do?*
-*What Would Jesus Do if He Dressed Like Urkel?*
-*7 Steps to a Hissy-Fit Free New Year*
-*Wake Up Baldy! Tough Love for Men Over 40*
-*Ask Me If I Care: The Five Words That Can Change Your Life*

For Children
-*Bingo, The Really, Really, Big Squirrel*
-*Suzie's Magic Manic-Depressive Lemonade*
-*Going To The Woods To Feed The Bears That Symbolize My Stepmom's Drinking Problem*
-*Loogie Luke, The Kid That Could Spit the Furthest*
-*The Pretty Unicorn and the Magic Spell of the Beverly Hills Surgeon*
-*From Caterpillar to Moth to X-Ray Vision Giant to Class Action Suit Against DuPont*
-*Mommy, Why Does Daddy Sleep in the Daytime?*

Attempt to win literary award
-*Sycamore Wind: New & Selected*

Acknowledgments

"Was it Hamlet wronged Laertes? Never Hamlet." Some of these works have previously appeared, in different forms, in *The Coast, Java Snob, Matrix, Mississippi Mud, Queen Street Quarterly, River City & Short Fuse*. "Grimace" is for Kevin Flynn and John McIntyre. "Batman" finishes with a commentary inspired by a poem by Tim Enman. Grateful thanks to Alicia Boutilier, Jason Camlot, John Fraser, Gary Hillier, Nick Lolordo, Scott Macdonald, Nick and Bernadette Mount, and Matthew Rosenberg. Thanks to Adrienne Ho for the photo-shoot. Cheers Jon Paul Fiorentino and Alessandro Porco for their valued insights and encouragements. Special thanks to Stephen Cain, Adrienne Weiss, Mike O'Connor and everybody at Insomniac Press. Thanks so much to Lynn, Jim, and Mary for laughing to some of these bits in their first form; to Janice, Johnny and Mike for always being there; for everybody in my family, esp. my wonderful and inspiring parents, John & Mary. To Carol, sweet sunshine.